Full Circle

Cherie K

notionpress.com

INDIA • SINGAPORE • MALAYSIA

Notion Press Media Pvt Ltd

No. 50, Chettiyar Agaram Main Road,
Vanagaram, Chennai, Tamil Nadu – 600 095

First Published by Notion Press 2021

ISBN 978-1-63997-684-3

CHAPTER 1

It was a scorching hot summer's afternoon in Delhi. The kind of heat that forced people indoors and drained out the whole energy out of you if you stepped out in the sun. In Satya Niketan, a colony in South Delhi, the streets were deserted except for a few hawkers selling cucumbers and young couples from nearby Venky's College walking hand in hand with the promise of young love. From the balcony of the small flat she lived in; Eva looked down into the narrow street. At 25, she was already a doctor with an MBBS degree preparing for the PG entrance exams necessary to clear so she can attach the magical MD to her name. But at the moment studies were the last thing on her mind; she was thinking of the lush greenery, the overcast skies and the never-ending rain of Shillong, her hometown. Standing there in the scorching Delhi heat, she missed her home with every fibre of her being.

The front door opened and startled her out of her reverie. Her roommate Nisha came in with Bhaskar, both flushed red and sweating profusely. Nisha made a beeline for the fridge and took out a bottle of water and took a deep swig. "Hey Eva, still missing the old college in Lucknow? Chill yaar, this is Delhi. Enjoy." Nisha was herself from Nainital and had been her friend since the beginning of their MBBS days. In those days, the fact that they were both from the hills had drawn the girls together and with time forged a deep bond between the two girls.

"So, are we going to RML tonight or not?" Nisha asked Eva.

"Oh! The party! I had forgotten all about it." Replied Eva when secretly her heart was pounding thinking about Debojit. Good-looking and dashing, he made her heart skip a beat each time he looked at her. He was intelligent and had been in Delhi for a year before Nisha and Eva had come to Delhi. He was preparing for the same exams, but he was working in the Ram Manohar Lohiya Hospital as a Junior Resident and staying in the hostel there. There are lots of junior doctors from the Northeast in RML, joining after they've completed their MBBS, with big dreams and aspirations of working in a big city. Debojit himself is from Guwahati. And tonight's party was in the hostel there.

Eva was thinking if she should cook something to take to the party as the boys in RML were both lousy and lazy cooks and drinks and snacks would be foremost on their minds, and of course as a bonus it might impress Debojit. She turned and smiled at Nisha saying, "Let's make some fried chicken for tonight." Nisha winked at her and remarked that they should let cardiac surgeons know that the way to a man's heart is through his stomach. The two girls giggled at the comment while Bhaskar shook his head. "You girls have eyes only for Debojit."

CHAPTER 2

Eva snapped back from her reverie with a chuckle. Now Dr Eva Lisa Lyngdoh, a Medical Specialist in a leading hospital in Shillong, her hometown, her life was a far cry from those days in Delhi. She smiled fondly as she remembered those days of hectic preparation and studying for a Post Graduate seat, a precious few that were available, and the competition was enormous. As she sat in her Clinic in a posh area of the town, she thought life had turned out well for her. A successful practice, a wonderful, loving and supportive husband and two lovely daughters, she felt she couldn't have asked for more. She finished her cup of tea and called for the next patient. But as she went about her work, there was a little thought niggling in the back of her mind as to why she remembered that exact day in Delhi after almost 12 years.

The afternoon passed swiftly by. Soon it was 6pm and she finished her last appointment and wrapped up for the day. In her car she checked her phone before driving. There were a bunch of Whatsapp notifications waiting. "Lord," she thought to herself, "I'll read them when I get home." They are usually some Medical Representatives' promotions on Whatsapp. She pulled out from the parking lot but there was a sense of unease. She kept glancing at her phone unable to focus on anything else. It was as if a voice was asking her to look at her messages. Her unease grew as she was in caught in the rush hour bumper-to-bumper traffic in Laitumkhrah. She got out of the rush and turned into the quietness of Risa Colony, where she lives. As soon as she stopped her car in her short driveway, she grabbed her phone and saw her Whatsapp. And there in the middle of the myriad messages was one from her MBBS group from college that closed around her heart in a grip of ice. "Dr Nisha Barthwal committed suicide." In a daze she scrolled and read the messages from her old batchmates, trying to glean more information. Nisha had been found dead, hanging in the bedroom of her house in Nainital. Her husband, Dinesh Pathak, had found her when he and their daughter returned grocery shopping from a nearby market.

She sat there in her car unable to move, hot tears spilling uncontrollably, thinking of her friend Nisha, with whom she had lost touch after moving out of Delhi to join her MD course. Nisha didn't clear the exam that year and had gone back to Nainital and never retuned her calls. She was not in the batch's Whatsapp group or on Facebook. Eva had come to know that she is a practicing Paediatrician in Nainital but since they have not kept in touch, she kept putting off trying to contact her. And now as she sat there, burdened with guilt and thinking about the might-have-beens, her mind wandered again into the past.

CHAPTER 3

"Wake up, Sleepyhead," Nisha's voice came from far away. Eva rolled over and opened her eyes. Nisha stood at the foot of the bed carrying two coffee mugs and the smell of fresh coffee brought Eva sitting up in bed. She smiled, because her friend was all jumpy and excited with the dreamy eyes of a newfound crush. The party in RML had been great. Debojit had spoken to the girls, but he seemed besotted with Nisha and soon the pair had gone for a walk leaving Eva with the others at the party. They returned after the party had broken up and Eva had gone to Mami's room to sleep. They had planned to stay overnight in the hostel as it wouldn't have been safe to go back to Satya Niketan at night. And as a bonus they got to have some late-night girl talks with Mami, their friend from Mizoram. But that night the girls didn't sleep at all as Nisha was overjoyed and excited that Debojit had asked them, meaning he asked her, but with the other two as camouflage, for a movie in PVR Priya, a hangout in south Delhi, the next day, as it was a Sunday. And so blossomed the innocent love between her two friends. In spite of the gruelling schedules of their studies, they found time to be together. When they were together it was as if the world around them ceased to exist.

As they were having coffee, Eva was thinking of the chapters lined up for the whole week that she was determined to finish. It was already July and she had planned on finishing the course for PG once by August so that she can concentrate and revise the more important topics and MCQ guidebooks from September. The course for Medical Post Graduate entrance was vast and at the end of the day everyone has to rely on the Guidebooks with the previous years' Multiple-Choice Questions with explanations. Many take a short cut and just read the Guidebooks, but it was a gamble Eva was not prepared to take. Cutting through her thoughts, Nisha was chattering away, her thoughts nowhere near studies, a foolish grin on her face. "I think I love him yaar. I know it's so sudden, but I can just feel it." So, the days went by, Eva laboriously studying the whole week with the weekends spent at RML, courtesy Nisha. For Nisha, on the other hand, it was a struggle between studying for the exams and spending time with her newfound love. And of course; love always won.

CHAPTER 4

It was late October, and the winter chill was beginning to set in. And with it came fervent revisions and a renewed passion to study as the various PG entrance exams are scheduled over the winter starting with AIIMS in November. The exam to the most prestigious institute in the country is one of the toughest but serves as a guide to how prepared a student is for all the other exams. For Eva, Nisha and countless doctors preparing, these months were crucial, and the days passed in a haze of caffeine induced late night studying. Each day seemed too short for the number of books they had to cram for the exams. Nisha, however, had other things on her mind as well. Things were not going well between her and Debojit. Of late she had started complaining to Eva that he seemed preoccupied and distant. That evening, since it was a Saturday, Eva asked Nisha if she was going out with Debojit. "No, yaar," replied Nisha. "I called him but he's not answering my call, Mr Grumpy-Grouchy that he is now. Let's order in, he can do as he pleases." Eva smiled at Nisha's tantrum. "He must be tense due to the exams. Everyone is tense now. Don't worry, things will be back to normal." So, they decided to order some Chinese food from a small restaurant in Satya Niketan, popular among college students.

"I'm going for a bath, Nisha. The delivery boy will call on my phone." Eva called out from the bathroom. She was in the middle of her bath when she heard her phone ring. Thinking hungrily about chicken fried rice, she was shocked to hear her friend scream. She quickly turned off the water, wrapped a towel around herself and went out. She found Nisha ashen, sitting with the phone clutched in her hand, someone rapidly talking at the other end. Eva took the phone. It was Mami at the other end. "Eva, you and Nisha come quickly. Something has happened. Debojit is not well." Eva could hear her sobbing as well as some commotion in the background. Fear clutched her heart in an icy grip. She felt a sense of foreboding. She turned to Nisha and saw her own fear mirrored in her friend's face. Eva managed a small smile for her friend even though inside she was sick with dread.

"What happened to Debojit? He must be really sick. It's my fault I ignored him all this while." Nisha sobbed.

"Let's not get ahead of ourselves;" replied Eva. "We'll go to RML and see. Don't worry, Nisha, everything will be okay."

The two of them got ready, and dinner forgotten, they got into an autorickshaw for RML Hospital. When they reached RML, they found quite a crowd gathered in front of the Doctors' Hostel. As they made their way inside, they heard the word suicide among the crowd. Anxious and filled with dread, they entered the building only to be stopped by the hostel security guard. However, Mami was waiting for them and took them to her room on the first floor. Another girl, Zuali, was in the room and John, a boy from Nagaland came in. There the whole story came out. It seems that everyone was busy studying the whole week, but since it was a Saturday, the boys had made plans to cook and have a few drinks. So, they had asked Mami and Zuali to cook chicken and John was helping the girls. At around 6 pm, Rahul and Saurav, both from Assam, knocked on Debojit's door saying, "Let's go to Gole Market to get some beer." There had been no answer, but they assumed he heard them and went to their own rooms to get ready. When, after half an hour of waiting he still didn't turn up, they went down to his room, room no. 250 on the second floor. Ready to bang on the door, they found it was ajar. Surprised, they pushed it open, and it was there that they found him. Hanging from the hook of the ceiling fan with a bedsheet around his neck, a chair overturned nearby. He had taken down his fan and tidied up his room meticulously. Shocked and frightened out of their wits, the two boys screamed for help. Other hostellers came running and on seeing what had happened there was immediate chaos. His friends wanted to take him down immediately and rush to the emergency; but others cautioned that they should inform the police first. So, Rahul called the police *chowki* in RML itself and soon the police came with a stretcher and took him to the ER where he was pronounced Dead on Arrival. Meanwhile, the Medical Superintendent had come with the police to the hostel and sealed the room. The police had a few questions for Rahul and Saurav as well as other friends and inmates of the adjoining rooms. The body had been taken to the mortuary awaiting post-mortem. The hospital authorities have informed his parents, but Saurav had called them but he had no answers to their sobbing cries of why this had happened.

Nisha listened to all this, weeping unconsolably. She turned to Eva and said, “Why did he do this? He could have talked to me. Or to any of us. We’re all here. We’re all his friends. I loved him so much. How could he not even say goodbye? “The others tried to console her, but she was inconsolable. Everyone was crying and in shock. Suicide is a terrible thing and when it happens to one of your own its hard to accept. A whole life snuffed out just like that. A friend, who till a few hours before, was making plans for the weekend was now lying cold on a mortuary table. Time passed by in a daze. Someone brought tea for them which they drank mechanically; hunger the last thing on their minds.

CHAPTER 5

Eva's mind jolted back to the present. Her husband Bantei, or Ban as she called him, had come out to see why she hadn't entered the house when he had heard her car awhile back. He saw her tears as she walked inside the house and was immediately concerned. "What happened? Are you hurt?" Eva shook her head. She collapsed in his arms and told him, "Nisha committed suicide. She hung herself." "Your college friend, Nisha?" Tearfully she nodded. "It's alright, baby. It's alright". He held her and stroked her hair. He led her to their bedroom and told her to freshen up and rest. He will take care of the kids and their dinner. "Don't worry, relax. I will attend to the kids. You just rest."

She washed her face, changed her clothes and got into bed. Ban came in with two mugs of fresh coffee. She then told him what had happened. How she came to know of Nisha's suicide through her MBBS Whatsapp group. "We were the best of friends, Ban. But she dropped off the grid after we left Delhi. Now it's too late." "Don't blame yourself darling," he replied. "Tomorrow morning, you call her husband. Talk to him. It will make you feel better." Eva then told him of how she had a kind of premonition of what was going to happen. Of how in the afternoon her mind wandered to the days in Delhi when Nisha and Debojit were together. Ban gave her a comforting smile, "These things happen: strange though it may seem, sometimes we have premonitions about what is about to happen." Ban was a loving husband, a kind soul, and Eva felt she was very lucky to have him as her husband. Good-looking and intelligent, he had completed his MBA from one of the top business schools in the country. After a stint working in one of the corporates in Mumbai, he had decided that the hectic schedule and stressful lifestyle of the corporate world was not his cup of tea. So, he had come back to Shillong and set up a successful clothing retail business. With two multi-brand stores and a branded showroom, he was doing quite well sans the stress of the corporate world. He had time for his family and could afford to pursue his hobby, cooking. A self-taught cook, or "chef" as he often corrected, he loved experimenting with new dishes and complex cuisines. Friends and family rarely ever refused dinner invites at their house as they were often treated to gastronomical experiences. Even now, as Eva was upset, he had whipped up a delicious Chinese stir fry for their dinner.

After dinner and the children had gone to bed, Eva sat at her laptop trying to find either Nisha's or her husband Dinesh's contact numbers in any of the doctors' websites. Her husband came and asked her, "What are you looking for?"

"Ban, I don't have Nisha's husband's number. I asked my batchmates if any of them had his number, but no one seems to know. I'm trying to search online but no such luck."

"Is he a doctor?" Asked Ban. "We can reach the hospital he's practicing and try to get his number. But darling, its late. We'll try calling in the morning. You should try to sleep. Tomorrow we'll try to get in touch with him somehow."

Eva got into bed, but sleep eluded her. She was overwhelmed with guilt. She thought about her MBBS days, when she first met Nisha, when they had been roommates. College had been a cultural shock for Eva. Everything was different and strange. The overwhelming heat of the Lucknow summers, the food, the environment. And to add to that, she didn't speak a word of Hindi in the beginning. She felt lost and often cried. Nisha had been her rock then. Translating for her when they went out shopping, teaching her Hindi at the same time. Nisha was the one she talked to when she felt homesick. Both of them used to study together and make fun of the teachers, gave them funny names which no one else understood. Eva mourned for her friend. And deep in her heart she somehow felt that Nisha's suicide had something to do with her past in RML. Her mind went back to that fateful night.

CHAPTER 6

Eva and Nisha stayed in RML for the night. They felt they couldn't return to their flat; both of them had been shaken to the core and they wanted to be near their friends. That no one slept a wink that night was not surprising. Everyone was in shock and kept on talking and discussing the turn of events. They kept on talking about Debojit, the friend that he was, memories of good times made them laugh through their tears only to be hushed into a grim silence when they realised he was no more. Morning came, and with it came the realisation that no one had eaten since the previous evening. Mami made tea and the boys went and ordered parathas from the hostel mess. The food came and as they were eating, Rahul asked, "Should we go and receive Uncle and Aunty from the airport?" Suddenly it hit home. Debojit's parents were coming on the morning flight from Guwahati and should be there by afternoon. The food turned to sawdust in their mouths when they thought of his parents, the grief they must be feeling. And Nisha was scared witless, ashamed to face them lest they blame her for what had happened. They decided that John and Rahul should go to the airport and accompany Debojit's parents to the hospital and whichever hotel they were staying.

Debojit's parents, Mr & Mrs. Bhowmick, came to the hostel around 4 p.m. They had finished the formalities with the hospital authorities and gone through the ordeal of viewing their son's body. They said they wanted to see the place where their son had spent his last days. So, the boys brought them to the hostel, to Mami's room. There they met Eva and Nisha and the rest of Debojit's friends. Rahul took them up to the second floor, and on seeing Room no. 250, Aunty collapsed in grief. She wept unconsolably. In Mami's room, the girls gave them tea and tried to talk to them, to give them whatever small comfort they could. Both of them said that Debojit never mentioned anything amiss whenever they spoke on the phone. In fact, they said, he sounded quite hopeful of clearing the exams. He had told them that he will be home in February or March after counselling is over and he would spend some time at home before joining PG. Tears streamed down Aunty's cheeks as she recounted this. "Why did he do something like this? If he had any problems, he could have told us. We would have always stood by him. Did he seem disturbed to any of you? Was he depressed?" John and Rahul replied, "No, Aunty. He never said anything to any of us. He was his usual self. Of course, all of us are tense for the exams, but it was nothing more than usual." Everyone fell silent. Each lost in their own thoughts. The parents lost in grief for their son, full of dreams and aspirations, now his life had been cut short by his own hand. If there had been a reason for his suicide, he had chosen to take it with him to the grave. His friends remembered the countless moments with him, studying together, going out for movies, the drunken escapades, trivial though they were, they made up precious memories. How he had always wanted to be a surgeon. Now everything was gone, their friend was gone. Nisha, mourned for her lost love. Though they had been together for a few months, both of them had been inseparable. And they had often talked about the future, made plans of trying to get PG in the same college, of building a life together.

Aunty's voice cut through her thoughts. "He told me that he was bringing a special girl home. Who is it?" Nisha's heart lurched. Her mind went blank. She didn't know what to say. But Eva came to her rescue. She told them that it was Nisha. Aunty got up and hugged her, tears rolling down her cheeks. Tears also flowed from Nisha's eyes and the two of them held each other mourning for the one person they both loved.

CHAPTER 7

The ringing alarm jolted Eva awake the next morning. She glanced at the clock. It was 7am. She felt tired, as if she hadn't slept at all. Which was almost true anyway. The night before both she and Nisha had come back to Satya Niketan. However, they couldn't sleep. Nisha kept crying and they both sat up till the sky had started to lighten with dawn. They finally slept at around 5:30 am. Eva got out of bed and found Nisha in the next room sitting on a chair staring grim and despondent at her phone. She was dry eyed with no more tears left, there was just a sense of hopelessness in her eyes. Eva went and sat down in front of her friend. "Nisha, I know you love him. And I cannot imagine the pain you are going through now. But you must pull yourself together. You have to be strong. We have to help Uncle and Aunty through all this. We have to help them take him home. Debojit would want that. And you have to show them that the girl their son loved is strong and matured, who they can depend on. Let them have a good memory of him."

"Eva, I'm scared they think that I might be the cause of his depression." "No, Nisha, I don't think they blame you. No one knows why he did it. Maybe, later when we go through his stuff, we might have a chance of understanding. But for now, keep it out of your mind. Pray to God to give you the strength to get through this." Nisha nodded listlessly but when Eva made tea and toast, she managed to eat a bit.

For all her talk, Eva was also no better. Her mouth was dry with worry, but she kept a brave front for her friend's sake. She was scared that Nisha would sink into depression. Or that she would try to harm herself. It was a kind of blessing that they were going to be busy the whole day. Mr & Mrs. Bhowmick had booked a room in a hotel in Paharganj and the girls were headed over there. The boys, Rahul, John and Saurav, would be accompanying Mr Bhowmick as he completed all the formalities so they can take their son's body home. The body had been transferred to the mortuary in AIIMS, and there was a lot of red-tape they had to navigate in order to be able to take it to Guwahati, especially since it was a medico-legal case.

The girls brought Mrs Bhowmick back to Satya Niketan. They couldn't leave her alone in the hotel, lost in grief as she was. Mami and Zuali were also coming to keep them company. When they reached home, Aunty seemed to find solace in talking to Nisha, so Eva left them talking softly to each other in her bedroom. Both seem to have exhausted their tears and were talking and slowly getting to know each other. The scene brought tears to Eva's eyes. Under normal circumstances it would have been a joyful thing that both of them got along so well, but now, it was a sad reminder of their loss. Eva and the other two girls, Mami and Zuali, set about preparing lunch, trying to bring some semblance of normalcy into the situation.

CHAPTER 8

Monday morning dawned with a slight nip in the air. Since the previous day was a Sunday, they couldn't finish the formalities required for Mr & Mrs Bhowmick to take their son's body back to Guwahati. Again, the boys set out with Uncle to get the various No-objection Certificates required from the Police and other departments. Eva and Zuali headed out to Connaught Place to one of the travel agencies there in order to book flight tickets for Mr & Mrs Bhowmick to return to Guwahati. They went to one of the big travel agencies there and explained the situation. The people at the agency were very helpful and explained the various procedures and certificates required. They also reassured the girls that they will handle the bookings, they need not worry. Eva and Zuali were relieved. If all went well, Uncle and Aunty could leave the very next day.

Next, they went to RML Hostel, they were told that Debojit's room had to be emptied and vacated. The girls were shocked. They sat in the Doctors' canteen and had coffee to clear their heads. Eva said, "Zuali, I don't think Uncle and Aunty would want to clear Debojit's things now." "Yes, and there are so many things in his room he might not want his parents to see." replied Zuali. Eva thought about the beer bottles, the ashtrays, the cigarette packs and shuddered. "After everything, its best his parents don't see the things in his room. We can volunteer to clean it later and send the stuff to them by cargo. They need not know about the parties, the drinking or the smoking. His parents deserve whatever good memories they have of him." Zuali agreed with her. So, they went to the hostel caretaker and asked for a weeks' time. However, the caretaker was a nice elderly man who knew all of them well. He told them that they need not worry, usually a period of 15 days was given to vacate the room. The girls heaved a sigh of relief.

When they reached Satya Niketan, they found Nisha in a relatively better mood. Mami had cooked lunch and Nisha even managed to eat a little. Aunty also ate a bit of rice and dal after Nisha begged her to eat. By evening, Uncle and the boys returned. They had completed all the formalities and had obtained all the certificates necessary to travel. Eva then called the travel agency and confirmed that Mr & Mrs Bhowmick would be leaving the next day.

The boys left with Uncle and Aunty, to drop them to their hotel. Mami and Zuali stayed behind in Satya Niketan. They all agreed to meet early the next morning at the AIIMS mortuary. The body had to be taken from there to the airport. And they all wanted to have a last look and say goodbye to their friend one last time.

After they left, there was a sense of emptiness. Throughout the day they had been busy, so it kept their thoughts and feelings at bay. Now as the four girls sat having tea, all the feelings of grief, anger, frustration and shock again came bubbling up. Even as they grieved for Debojit, they couldn't help feeling frustrated and angry at how he left them with no answers. Nisha also felt betrayed he didn't confide in her and he went and took the extreme step. Why he did so will always remain unanswered for the rest of her life. The thought that tomorrow will be the last time they said goodbye to their friend crushed them. They all felt a sense of loss and emptiness which cannot be put into words.

CHAPTER 9

The next morning, Eva woke up at 5am. She couldn't sleep after that. She kept thinking of the day ahead. By 7am, she gave up trying to sleep and got up to make a cup of coffee for herself. As she was busy in the kitchen, Zuali came in. "We couldn't sleep," she said. "From 4am, we were awake and talking. It's strange to think that today will be Debojit's last journey home." They made coffee and took it out to Nisha's room. No one felt like having breakfast. Thoughts of the day ahead filled everyone with a sense of dread.

The four girls were supposed to meet Mr & Mrs Bhowmick at the mortuary of AIIMS at 9am. The boys were coming with Uncle and Aunty. They quickly got dressed and by eight, were ready to leave. It was still early as Satya Niketan was not very far from AIIMS but there was a restlessness in them, they couldn't sit waiting anymore. They just wanted to get out of the flat.

As they sat in the autorickshaw on their way to AIIMS, each girl was lost in her own thoughts. Nisha was subdued and the pain she felt was mirrored in her face. Eva was worried for her friend. She prayed Nisha would find enough strength to face the day ahead.

When they reached AIIMS, the boys had not yet arrived, so they sat in the shade to wait. Eva felt that it was her mood or the circumstances around her, but it seemed as if the air was heavy with melancholy, as if a quiet sadness enveloped them as they waited. Soon the boys arrived with Mr & Mrs Bhowmick. All three boys faces showed a grim sadness, as if the pain bottled up inside was too much too bear. Yet each face also showed a quiet determination, prepared to complete these last few tasks, so their friend can begin his last journey home.

Uncle went inside with Saurav and John to complete the paperwork, while Rahul waited outside with Aunty and the girls. After a while, Aunty was called inside for viewing the body. Aunty's face paled, and trembling, she turned to the girls, "Please come with me. I cannot do this alone." You are not alone Aunty," replied Mami. "All of us will come with you." So, the four girls walked alongside Aunty on what was perhaps the hardest walk of her life. Inside, when they saw their son's body, prepared and dressed inside the coffin, both Uncle and Aunty broke into tears. The girls too couldn't control themselves and they all cried as they said goodbye to their friend one last time. Nisha placed a single red rose on his chest and came away sobbing. The boys too said their goodbyes. Soon it was time to close the coffin and seal it for transport.

After everything was done, at last it was time to finish the grim journey to the airport. Uncle and Aunty had booked a cab, so the girls and Aunty went in the cab while Uncle and the boys accompanied the body in the mortuary van. The flight to Guwahati was at 3pm and they were supposed to reach the airport at least three hours ahead to complete the formalities. They were flying by Jet Airways and Uncle had already called ahead. He had already been assured that someone from the airline will meet them at the departure lounge. They reached the airport, and, as promised, a Jet Airways staff was waiting for them. He efficiently took the papers required, checked their tickets and promised both Mr & Mrs Bhowmick that he will take care of everything.

The time had come to say goodbye to Uncle and Aunty. Uncle looked at them, his pain written on his face. “I cannot find words to thank all of you for helping us and being with us in this time of tragedy. And above all thank you for the friendship you have shown my son. For the love you have given him both when he was alive, and now after he is no longer with us.” Uncle trembled and continued, “You have shown us that no matter what demons my son faced that caused him to take his life, at least he had friends who loved him. We will never know the reason he had done this, but we can find solace in the fact that you all loved him till the end.”

Nisha could no longer control herself, she cried, and Aunty hugged her and said, “Nisha, you and Debojit loved each other. You are the daughter-in-law we will never have. You are welcome to visit us anytime you want.” She looked at the others and said, “All of you are welcome to visit us. Whenever you find yourselves in Guwahati, our home is yours. We will never forget these past few days. We were lost and beyond grief, but you all helped us through.” She hugged each one of them. Tears were flowing through everyone’s eyes as they said their final goodbyes and entered the airport.

CHAPTER 10

Eva woke up late the next morning. She hadn't been able to sleep as her mind dwelt in the past. All her memories of what had happened in Delhi had been so much alive in the night, she felt a sense of dèjà vu. She had drifted off to sleep in the wee hours of the morning. Now she glanced at her bedside clock, it was 9am. Her husband Ban had already gotten up and must have have gone for his morning run. Ban liked to keep fit and he ran every morning and worked out at the gym at least three to four times a week. She quickly got up, freshened up and went to the kitchen. She refused to let her mind dwell on the previous day's events, as she had to see to her daughters' breakfast.

"Good morning Mummy," they both chimed, and rushed to kiss her. Amanda was six years old and Clarissa four. Eva hugged them, thankful for her good fortune. She ruffled their hair and asked, "What do my darlings want for breakfast?" "Maggi," came the prompt reply.

"Hmm, girls, you know Maggi is not for breakfast," Ban said from the door. He had just returned from his morning run. "I'll tell you what, let's make French toast, give Mummy a treat." He winked at Eva amid happy grins from the girls. They loved helping him cook. Deng, their helper, bustled off to clean and mop. Eva made tea for herself and Ban and heated milk for the girls. Soon the family sat down for breakfast.

"Mummy, you're not going to the clinic today?" asked Clarissa.

"I am, sweetheart." Eva replied.

"But you were sick yesterday. Papa told us not to disturb you as you were having a headache."

"I'm alright now, darling. You both be good girls and come in the evening with Papa and we'll go and out for burgers."

After breakfast, Eva dropped the girls for piano lessons at the house next door. When she returned Ban told her there was a call for her. "Whoever it is had called three times. Must be something important. I was busy trying to call the hospital in Nainital where you said Nisha's husband is working."

"Did you get the number?" Eva asked excitedly.

"The reception said they don't give out doctors' personal numbers and I tried to talk to the MS but it's too early. I'll try again after an hour." Replied Ban.

At that moment her phone rang. Eva saw it was the same number which had called earlier. She answered.

"Is this Dr Eva Lyngdoh?" said an unfamiliar voice. "Yes," she replied, thinking it was a patient.

"I'm Nisha's husband, Dinesh."

Eva stood stunned.

"You must have heard about what had happened," said Dinesh, his voice raw with anguish.

"Yes, Dinesh, I'm so sorry. I can only imagine the grief you're feeling. If there is anything I can help with, please tell me."

"I don't know how to begin. But yesterday evening, after Nisha's last rites were completed, I had come back home. I was sitting at her desk when I saw something tucked inside a book. It was an envelope addressed to you. I didn't want to give it to the police. I felt she wanted me to give it to you. So, I called up a few colleagues in Lucknow and was able to get your number from one of your batchmates. Should I send it to you?"

Eva was shocked beyond words. She had lost touch with Nisha, but her friend had left a final message for her. Tears welled up in her eyes, and she told Dinesh, "Let me talk with my husband. I'll call you back."

Eva disconnected the call and turned to her husband, who was already looking expectantly at her. "Ban, that was Nisha's husband on the phone. He said she left a letter addressed to me, and he had not turned that to the police."

"I wonder why she had left a letter for you." He replied.

"I wonder if she had written something about why she took this extreme step. Dinesh asked if he should send me the letter, but I don't think he should post it."

"Eva, do you realize if there is something in that letter that implicates someone, we would have to turn it over to the police. If you can take a few days off from your practice, I think we should go to Nainital to see that letter."

"But the children?"

"We can ask Wanda to come and stay for a few days," Ban replied. Wanda was Ban's younger sister. She taught History at a local college while pursuing her PhD from NEHU, a prestigious university located in Shillong. The girls loved her and were always excited whenever she came over to stay.

"What about you, darling? Can you afford to take time away from your work?" Eva asked her husband.

He smiled. "That's the beauty of running your own business. You can always take time off. Besides, it will be only for a few days and it's important for us to go. So why don't you call up Dinesh and we can arrange to go whenever its convenient for him."

So, Eva called Dinesh and told him of their plan to visit Nainital. However, Dinesh had a different idea. "It would be convenient if you can come after two weeks. By then all the ceremonies would be complete. But Eva, I don't think you should come to Nainital. People talk, and Meera, our daughter is deeply affected by her mother's death. It would just lengthen matters and hurt her more. I can come up to Delhi and give you the letter."

"Of course, Dinesh. What you say is true. We'll meet in Delhi. When we've booked our flights and hotel, I'll let you know."

Eva put down her phone and turned to Ban, "He says we should meet in Delhi in two weeks. Nisha's *shradh* ceremony will be over and he will come to Delhi to give us the letter. Poor guy. People must be making it quite the scandal and it will only fuel speculation if we go there. He's worried for his daughter Meera."

"I agree," her husband replied. "Rumour mongers will have a field day if we turn up in Nainital."

So, everything agreed, both of them got ready to go to work.

CHAPTER 11

The next two weeks were whirlwind of activity. They arranged for Ban's sister Wanda to stay with the girls. She was happy to do so, and the girls were delighted at the prospect of their aunt staying over. Or as they put it, an adventure without Mummy and Papa. But Eva had to make sure all their medications were available in the house. And she set out different sets of clothes for the girls, for she knew they were active and might want to go for outings with their aunt. She knew selecting outfits for the girls would drive Wanda crazy. It often drove her crazy as it is. Then she called Deng, their helper, and took inventory of the kitchen supplies. Afterwards it was a trip to the market to get fresh groceries. Ban told her, "Darling, its ok. Wanda can manage." Eva knew she was going overboard, but this was going to be the first time both of them were going away together. Usually, one of them stayed with the kids if they had to go out of town. And since both of them were going she couldn't help but worry a bit, even though she knew the girls were in good hands with Ban's sister.

Eva was busy in her clinic too. Her patients' appointments had to be rescheduled. And there were some patients who wanted to come in for a check-up before she left. Her days became more hectic because she had to adjust them along with her normal appointments. Eva usually planned her trips so she could adjust appointments beforehand. Abrupt absences were a bit of a problem, so she avoided them except in dire emergencies. She also had to arrange for someone to take her ward rounds in the hospital.

Ban was also busy arranging things with his staff so he can leave for Delhi. "Eva," said Ban as he picked her up from her clinic in the evening for grocery shopping, "maybe I can visit some whole sellers in Delhi while we're there, get a bit of business done, kill two birds with one stone?"

Eva looked at her husband, ever the businessman, "Let's see if we have time."

It was late October and Ban was planning ahead for the festive season as business in clothing retail boomed during the months before Christmas.

"Have you booked the tickets Ban?"

"Yes, darling, already done. We're flying Jet Airways on Sunday morning, just five days from now. But I hadn't booked any return flight. I thought since we are going there, I might scout the markets a bit. And you too need a break after all this. Perhaps we can do some shopping for the girls."

In spite of everything, Eva relaxed, grateful to have such a loving and understanding husband. She felt better and began to make plans to do a bit of shopping for bags and make-up especially since few brands were available in Shillong. Little did she know of the surprise awaiting her in Delhi.

CHAPTER 12

Their bags were packed and were in the lobby waiting to be loaded into the car. Eva and Ban came downstairs hugging both their daughters goodbye. Eva held back her tears. It was hard to say goodbye to her daughters even if it was for a few days. The girls, however, were excited at the prospect of staying with Wanda, their aunt. Clarissa was a bit downcast but cheered up when her sister Amanda told her Mummy and Papa will come back with presents.

"Is that true Mummy?" she asked.

"Yes, sweetheart. You be good girls. Listen to Aunt Wanda and we will be back in no time with lots of presents."

Eva kissed both of them and hugged Wanda. Ban hugged the girls hard and told his sister, "Any problem just call us. Take care." Then they both got into the waiting car which will take them to the airport in Guwahati. It was a three hours' drive if the traffic was light. As they drove away Eva looked back and waved, tears forming in her eyes.

"Don't worry, they will be alright. In fact, if I know my sister, they will have so much fun, they won't have the time to miss us."

Eva looked at her husband with a wry smile, "But I miss them already."

They stopped for lunch at Nongpoh, a small town along the Guwahati-Shillong Highway where all the taxis and cars halted for food and snacks. The drive brought back memories to Eva. How many times she had travelled along this road during her college days. The long drives to the airport, the flights to Delhi, then the morning journey from Delhi to Lucknow by the Shatabdi Express. She was usually exhausted by the time she reached the hostel. But Nisha would be waiting and both girls would tell each other stories of their vacation at home while gorging on home cooked goodies. But this time she hardly noticed the beautiful scenery flashing by. She never imagined she would be making this journey under the present circumstances. Nisha found dead with a letter addressed to her. Those carefree hostel days seemed a lifetime away.

CHAPTER 13

After an uneventful flight they landed in Delhi in the early evening. Ban had made reservations in a five-star hotel in New Friends Colony and arranged for a pick-up from the hotel. They didn't want the hassle of getting a cab from the airport to the hotel. After they had checked in, and reached their room, Eva was totally exhausted. However, she called Dinesh, Nisha's husband and arranged to meet the next morning at Select City Walk, a posh mall in Saket.

"Eva, do you want to go out for a while, maybe have dinner outside?" Ban asked as he emerged from the bathroom after taking a shower. "We can go to Connaught Place, your favourite hangout, browse through a few shops, and then have dinner. It will do you good. Otherwise, you will sit and worry about tomorrow morning."

Eva smiled. Her husband knew her too well. If they stayed in, she would just worry about tomorrow, about the girls back home, about the past. "Sounds like a good idea Ban. Why don't you call up room service for coffee and something to eat? In the meantime, I'll shower and get ready."

By the time she finished her shower the coffee and sandwiches had arrived. The sandwiches were artfully arranged, and the aroma of coffee filled the room. She realised was famished. They soon finished their coffee and got ready to leave. The hotel had arranged for their car rental, and when they came out, the found a Honda Amaze waiting for them at the entrance. Eva looked at Ban, "You are really splurging on this trip. The hotel, the car, both must've cost a pretty penny."

Ban gave a sheepish grin, "We deserve a break. And since the reason for our trip is so grim, I think some creature comforts are welcoming. Besides, we can afford it."

Eva nodded, her heart overflowing with love for her husband. It sometimes amazed her how the two of them often do not require words to communicate. Their thought processes were almost identical.

In Connaught Place, they walked hand in hand, enjoying the mild evening. Thankfully in October, Delhi's fierce summer heat had abated. Though it was still hot in the daytime, especially for them coming from Shillong where summer temperature rarely goes above 26 degrees Celsius, the evenings were pleasant. For Eva, CP was a delight. The bright lights, the branded showrooms, the old-world charm of Connaught Place, she found herself filled with nostalgia for the old days when they used to come to CP for walks and window shopping and hanging out. The bright posh malls of Gurgaon and Saket could never beat a shopping experience in CP. Everyone is unhurried, young people sitting around the benches, the place had a class of its own. And the Central Park in the middle was a green peaceful oasis. Sitting in the park, no one would ever dream that deep underneath the ground was the big bustling busy Metro station of Rajiv Chowk.

They strolled around, Eva buying a few things. "You seem to be enjoying yourself." Ban teased her.

Eva smiled, "Yes, darling. This is one of my favourite places in the world. Whenever I feel down or depressed, I used to come here, and my mood used to improve dramatically."

"Maybe it's the retail therapy?" her husband suggested mischievously.

"Maybe," agreed Eva with a twinkle in her eyes.

Very soon however, the fatigue of the journey caught up with them and they decided to have dinner and then head back to the hotel. Ban wanted to go to KFC. Eva was horrified. "Why KFC? We can get KFC back in Shillong. We've come all the way to Delhi, and you want to eat KFC??"

Finally, they decided on Bercos, a delightful Chinese restaurant in the middle circle which Eva remembered from the old days. The food was superb, and they thoroughly enjoyed their meal. They then went back to the hotel where they instantly fell into an exhausted sleep the moment they climbed into bed.

CHAPTER 14

The next morning Eva woke up with a sense of trepidation. She was worried about meeting Dinesh, the letter foremost in her mind. They had arranged to meet in a café in Select City Walk. She and Ban showered and dressed and went down for breakfast. Even though the breakfast buffet was sumptuous, Eva found she had no appetite. She settled for toast and coffee while Ban indulged himself in bacon, sausage, toast and fried egg, a heart attack on a plate. They finished their breakfast and took a walk along the swimming pool, taking pictures and video calling Amanda and Clarissa. Both girls were excited at the sight of the pool and wanted to stay in the same hotel for their next vacation.

By ten-thirty, Eva couldn't bear to wait any longer. They left for Saket and soon reached the busy mall. They walked around buying a few gifts to take back with them. Then Eva received a text from Dinesh to wait for him at a café in the adjoining DLF Mall. They reached the café. Dinesh had not arrived yet, so they sat down and ordered cold coffees. The café had an enchanting décor with a whole wall comprised of vintage doors. They had a table near the entrance from where they could see the escalators as well as the Hard Rock Café sign. They sat sipping their drinks, watching people pass by. Though her stomach was knotted with tension, Eva couldn't help marvelling at the anonymity of Delhi. Here they sat in the café, people milling about. Most were fashionable and carried branded shopping bags, yet everyone seemed oblivious of each other. Eva found such anonymity thrilling. Back home mostly people knew each other, and you can hardly walk ten paces without meeting someone you know. Of course, it gave you a sense of belonging, a feeling of security in a city you have grown up in but sometimes the anonymity of a big city gave a feeling of freedom, of being part of a crowd.

Soon Eva spotted Dinesh coming up on the escalator. They hadn't met before, but she recognised him from his Whatsapp picture. He came up to them and asked, "Dr Eva? I'm Dr Dinesh Pathak." Eva nodded, "Call me Eva, and this is my husband Ban."

The introductions were a bit awkward given the circumstances. However, they soon warmed up to each other given the close ties they had to Nisha. Over coffee, Dinesh narrated how he came back from the market with Meera, their daughter and found Nisha hanging in the bedroom.

"I was paralysed with shock. I don't recall doing it, but I must've pushed Meera away. I closed the door and called the neighbours. After they came, we called the police."

"Eva, I still cannot understand why she did this. Of course, for the past two or three months she had been a bit moody, but whenever I asked if there was anything wrong, she always said it was nothing just work stress. We were planning a trip to Goa in December."

"And she always talked about you. She said you were best friends, sisters almost. She kept track on where you were practicing. Many times, I told her to call you, but she would brush it off. I once asked her if the two of you had had some falling out, but she said no, it was just that she hadn't kept in touch all these years, she felt it would be awkward to suddenly call."

Eva teared up as she listened. Her heart swelled with emotion as she heard her best friend had always remembered her. "Dinesh, I always thought of Nisha. Many times, I wanted to contact her, but she was entirely off the grid. I searched for her in Facebook and other social media, but she was not online. I came to know of her suicide from our MBBS Whatsapp group."

"Yes," replied Dinesh. "She never liked to be on social media. She said she wanted her life to remain private. But she valued your friendship. She always said that Eva always understood, she had always been there for me."

"I wasn't too surprised when I found a letter in your name. It made sense that in the final days of her life she would reach out to you."

So saying, Dinesh took out a plain white envelope and gave it to Eva. Tears welled up when she saw her name written in Nisha's handwriting on the envelope. She would have have recognised it anywhere. She felt as if her friend was calling out to her from beyond this world. Ban put his arm around her shoulder and give it a quick squeeze. She was glad of his quiet reassurance. She took the envelope from Dinesh and was about to open it when he stopped her. "Eva, my wife must've had a reason that she left you a sealed envelope. Maybe there are things she wanted to confide in you. Let us respect her wishes. Please open it in and read it in private. If there are things you feel you should share with me, then you can call me and tell me."

That moment Eva felt a respect for this quiet man. Even in such a time of personal anguish he respected his wife's wishes. Even though Nisha had committed suicide without saying a single word, without a goodbye, and had thrown his whole life in a turmoil, he still loved her so much so as not to intrude into her personal space even after her death. Eva realised Dinesh was a gentleman and she made up her mind to read the letter and share the contents with him if possible.

They had long finished their coffees, but Dinesh seemed reluctant to leave. He seemed relieved to be able to talk about Nisha with people who understood her, who wouldn't judge her. Whenever he talked to people about his wife, he felt them judging him, their eyes blaming him for her suicide even though no one said it outright. With Eva and Ban, talking about Nisha gave him an inner peace, a sense of comfort for the first time since that fateful evening.

It was getting late. They had been sitting in the café for almost two hours. Dinesh was embarrassed he had talked so much, but Eva reassured him that it was alright. Ban even invited Dinesh to have a late lunch with them thinking that Dinesh might not want to be alone. Dinesh however, refused. "I'll go and meet some relatives in Safdarjung Enclave. You call me after you read the letter."

On the way back to the hotel Ban asked Eva if she wanted to eat somewhere but Eva's mind was elsewhere.

The letter seemed heavy in her handbag, and she wanted to read what her friend had to say to her in her final moments. "Ban, let's go back and just order something from room service." One look at his wife's face told Ban she needed time alone to read the letter. So, he put his arm around her and called their driver. They drove back to their hotel in silence. Eva mind was far away. She was thinking of what must have happened which made Nisha take such a drastic step. Dinesh seemed to be a nice person. Surely, she could've talked to him. But little did she know that things were far more complicated than that. That the reason for Nisha's death was something she could never have guessed.

CHAPTER 15

Eva lay on the bed and took out the letter. Again, she had a feeling that Nisha was reaching out to her from beyond the grave. It made the hair on her arms stand-on-end, and she gave a little shiver. She opened the envelope and saw the letter covered in Nisha's neat handwriting.

Dearest Eva,

My friend, my sister. If you're reading this then I am already dead, finally at rest from all the burdens of this world. I know you may find it strange that I chose you to write my final words even though we have not spoken for years. It is through no fault of yours that I haven't contacted you after we left Delhi. Through the years I missed your friendship, your company. But there are many secrets in my life which have prevented me from reaching out to you. For many years my life has been a lie; to myself, to my husband and my daughter Meera. I know I'm rambling, and you must be thoroughly confused by now. Let me start at the beginning.

It all started in Delhi when we were preparing for our PG exams. Remember we had gone for a party in RML Hostel and Debojit and I had fallen madly in love with one another? Well, Debojit and I were planning a future together. We had planned to get married as soon as he got an MS seat, and he was planning to introduce me to his parents that February after the exams. However, that was not to be so. He sadly took his own life without a word to me. The day after his parents had taken him home, I checked my email and found he had mailed me just before his death. He said he couldn't take the pressure anymore. He felt the pressure of PG selection was too much and he couldn't even look at his books anymore. When he stayed in his room, he felt as though the four walls were closing in, trapping him and he was unable to escape. He was truly depressed, and he begged me not to tell anyone about this, not to shame him after his death. So, I kept quiet. But two weeks after that, I missed my period. I was frightened but I couldn't confide in anybody, not even you. I took a pregnancy test and found out I was pregnant. I can't describe my feelings then. I coudn't tell anybody as I felt I owed it to Debojit. He had begged me not to shame him after his death. Part of me was scared and a part of me was elated to have a part of him growing inside of me. Of course, I never thought of undergoing an abortion. I wanted to have his baby.

I went home just after the exams and told my parents of what had happened. To say they were angry would be an understatement. They threatened to throw me out of the house. I returned to Delhi determined I would find a job to support myself and the baby. However, I realised I couldn't work in Delhi as many people in the medical fraternity knew me. I wanted to keep Debojit's last wish. Looking back, I realise now it had been a mistake. But at the time I wasn't thinking clearly. After you got a PG seat, I felt I should not burden you with my troubles. So, I applied for a job in a mission hospital in small town in UP. I did not tell them the truth; I doubt I would have gotten a job if they knew my story. So, I told them I was married, and my husband had gone to the UK and that I was working and saving money to join him. I was happy working there as my pregnancy progressed. However, I was extremely scared and worried about the future. As soon as I had the baby I would have to stop working for a few months. I was not financially stable to cope with that and I was constantly thinking about the future. I was all alone and terrified. I didn't dare approach my parents and I didn't have the courage to call any of my friends. I had not told anyone the truth since the beginning, so I felt ashamed to ask for help. I became increasingly depressed. At that time there was an elderly lady working as a nurse in the hospital, she had the same surname as yours, Lyngdoh, Mrs Lin Lyngdoh. She was from Meghalaya too. I guess that was what drawn me to her. She had a daughter who lived with her husband in Allahabad. Her daughter is a gynaecologist who had a private practice and she had settled with her husband in Allahabad. Mrs Lin was kind to me and took care of me. Slowly, having no one to turn to, I confided in her. I told her of my predicament. When I told her we both cried, and she hugged me and told me it's alright. We'll find a way. Being at my wits end, I decided to give up my baby for adoption. It tore my heart, but I was too young, lacking the maturity to make the right decisions. So, I told Mrs Lin what I had planned. Mrs Lin was appalled at the idea, however when we couldn't find any other way, she understood. Then just before the baby was born, she offered to take the baby and raise it herself. She told me she had an only daughter who is settled in Allahabad. She had no other children to take care of her and when she returned home to her village in Meghalaya, she would be alone in her old age relying on nephews and nieces to take care of her. She said this baby was God's answer to her prayers. She will raise and love it as her own. I was grateful. I didn't want my baby to end up with strangers. I loved and trusted Mrs Lin. When my time came, she took me to Allahabad and paid for my hospitalisation in a nursing home. I gave birth to a beautiful and sweet baby girl. I held her in my arms, tears of joy pouring down my cheeks. But it was not for long. I stayed with Mrs Lin and my daughter for a month. After that I left for Delhi and started preparing for PG once again. I never contacted Mrs Lin again. It was too painful, and I knew if I had called her, I would never have been able to stay away from my daughter. As you know I became a Paediatrician. I guess the longing for my daughter drew me towards children. Eventually I got married to Dinesh, a wonderful person and I had another daughter, Meera. But I never forgot my baby, the one I had given away. It tore my heart, and I never forgave myself for what I had done. I never told anyone about my past, not even Dinesh. Every day I went through my life normally, yet my conscience was heavy. I never knew any real happiness, I felt I was living a lie. I couldn't tell Dinesh about the past. I knew I was deceiving him too, but I couldn't find a way to tell him without forever ruining his life and happiness. I couldn't continue anymore. As the years passed, I became more and more overcome with guilt. Each moment of my life I regretted what I had done, and I was scared my past would catch up with me. I felt I have no right to ruin my husband and my daughter's life. It wasn't their fault. Dinesh loved me with all his heart; I was the one who deceived him. All these thoughts made me realise that my death is the only solution. I pray God forgives me for this and I find happiness in the afterlife.

Eva, please forgive me, my dearest friend. The reason I am writing to you is because you are the only person who understood me. We had formed a bond greater than friendship. We were sisters. Please try to find my daughter. I want to right all the wrongs in my life. I realise that I shouldn't have given her away. She is Debojit's flesh and blood. I should have at least spoken to his parents and let them take a decision. Please, my friend. I could not do this myself as I would have had to tell my husband. I wanted to spare him the hurt. Please try to find my daughter and unite her with Debojit's Mum and Dad. This is my last request to you.

And please forgive me. And please explain to Dinesh. Tell him everything. And ask him to forgive me if he can find it in his heart to do so.

Your friend and sister,

Nisha

PS: Mrs Lin's daughter's address

Dr Margaret L Singh, Ladies' Clinic, Tagore Town, Allahabad.

CHAPTER 16

Eva finished reading the letter. Tears were flowing down her cheeks. She was stunned at what she had read. Never for a moment had she ever suspected that her friend was in such dire straits. If only she had known. She felt an overwhelming sadness for Nisha. How lonely and desperate she must have been to give away her baby like that. She was young and immature, and life had dealt her a huge blow. Eva could only imagine how terrified her friend was. If only she had called, Eva would have told her at least to try and contact Debojit's parents. But sometimes life is not so easy. Poor Nisha had carried such a huge burden of guilt in her life, it had ultimately led her down the same path as Debojit. And now she had entrusted Eva with the responsibility of finding her daughter. Eva was shocked and couldn't begin to comprehend how to begin the search. She wanted to discuss everything with her husband. However, Ban had gone for a walk in the hotel grounds to give her privacy to read her letter. As she waited for him, Eva was lost in thought; about the past about how she should tell Nisha's husband Dinesh and then how she could possibly fulfil the responsibility Nisha had given her.

Ban came back and the first thing he saw was Eva's tear-stained face. "Are you alright, honey?" He asked, concern in his voice. Eva nodded, unable to speak, not knowing where to begin. Ban came over to the bed and hugged her letting her cry. After some time, she calmed down and told him the whole story, ending with how Nisha had asked her to find her daughter.

"Oh Ban, I don't know how to begin. And what if Debojit's parents don't want to have anything to do with the baby? And we don't even know if they are still alive. And they might not believe us. I'm so worried."

"Hush, darling. Don't worry so much. We will try to get in touch with that doctor in Allahabad. Find out where the child is. Then we will try to contact Debojit's parents."

"I think we should go to Allahabad, Ban. Some things are better dealt in person."

"Yes, I agree. But we should get in touch with Dinesh. He must be waiting to hear from us."

"That's another problem. How do we tell Dinesh? What do we even tell him? He would be destroyed to learn that Nisha hid such a big thing from him."

"Eva, I think you said Nisha wanted to right all the wrongs in her life. So, her husband deserves to know this. He deserves an answer as to why Nisha took her own life. All this started years ago with Debojit's suicide, and Dinesh just got caught up in what had happened. I think this story should end here. There has been enough sadness and hurt. It's time for the truth, for closure. Let's see what happens. I believe it will all work out."

"But Ban, I don't know how to tell Dinesh without hurting him."

"Eva, just let him read the letter. It would be better that he reads Nisha's words for himself. It would be easier than hearing it from someone else."

Eva then called Dinesh and told him they would meet him in the same café they met earlier. They agreed to meet at eleven thirty the next day. After the call, Eva called home and spoke to her daughters. Both were chirping excitedly, asking when Mummy and Papa would be back, and what presents they were bringing. Hearing their voices brought a smile to her face. She told them to be good and study. Ban then spoke to the girls. As she listened on, Eva was extremely grateful for the life she had. She couldn't help thinking about Nisha and how badly everything turned out for her.

CHAPTER 17

Eva couldn't sleep the whole night. She lay in bed remembering the incidents in Delhi years ago. In her mind she relived those terrible days twelve years ago when Debojit had committed suicide. She couldn't help but feel a deep sense of sadness for all that had happened. They were so young and carefree those days in Delhi. All of them had just completed their MBBS, all were freshly minted doctors working in Delhi with good salaries. They felt the world was their oyster. All of them had big plans for the future, heady plans of becoming big consultants in their own fields, of opening nursing homes or pursuing a career in a medical college, though everything hinged on getting through the one of the various PG entrance exams. So, they had all prepared hard for the exams, but no one had ever imagined a tragedy like this would unfold in their midst. After Debojit's suicide, everyone had been shaken to the core but with all the exams coming up, they had adapted. In a way it was a blessing. Everyone was focused on their studies it gave them little time to brood. But no one had suspected that it had been a greater tragedy for Nisha. Not even Eva who was her roommate.

Eva recalled that Nisha was listless and hardly talked but she thought it was because she loved Debojit and he gone so suddenly without a goodbye. She never suspected her friend was holding back such a huge secret. Looking back, she realised that Nisha hardly ate anything those days and always complained of gastritis. Now she understood it had all been signs of her early pregnancy. Eva silently berated herself for not being more attentive.

They had all skipped the AIIMS exams in early November that year except Eva. The shock of Debojit's sudden death had shaken all of them to the core. And the boys Rahul, John and Saurav had packed up Debojit's belongings and sent them by cargo to his parents. Eva, Zuali, Mami and Nisha too had helped. But it had been Nisha who had sorted and packed his clothes and shoes. She had sat in his room alone, sorting through his clothes saying that it was her way of saying goodbye to him, of feeling a connection to him one last time. They had all understood and gave her the space she needed. When everything was packed, they had cleaned his room and then gave the key to the hostel caretaker. Nisha had seemed lost, the grief in her too great. The tears had long dried up leaving behind a pain that could be seen in her eyes. But everyone had gone on with their lives assuming that with time Nisha's pain would heal. No one had imagined that those events of twelve years back would haunt Nisha for the rest of her life and ultimately lead her to the same fate.

By December everyone was studying in earnest, staying up late at night, fuelled by endless cups of coffee. Zuali and Mami and the boys came to Satya Niketan for studying and discussions. They found they could not concentrate in the hostel, haunted by the memories of Debojit. Many times, the boys slept on matresses in the living room. Everyday heated discussions of the exam topics led to more fervent revisions as after each discussion everyone felt they have not studied enough. And through all this, Eva now realised, no one noticed Nisha's pain. No one noticed the turmoil she must've gone through. Of course, given the pressure of exams and the fact that they all were young and immature, and also spooked by Debojit's death, Eva couldn't help wondering that maybe, if that had paid a little attention to Nisha, she would still be alive now.

After the exams, Nisha had gone home for a few days. Eva now understood she had gone to talk to her parents. When she returned, she didn't say anything about her trip home. Both she and Eva joined as junior residents in a private hospital in Pusa Road, to gain some experience while they were waiting for the results. The others too had started working in different hospitals in Delhi. These jobs were just temporary, a stop gap. If they cleared the exams, then they would join their courses and it would be a big step in their careers. If they didn't clear the exams, it was either back to square one and begin preparation again for the next year or go after a government job as a Medical Officer. All this while, Eva noticed Nisha was putting on a bit of weight, they even teased her that she was becoming fat. Nisha used to laugh it off saying she needed to exercise and burn off the winter fat. Eva never imagined it was because she was pregnant.

Soon the results were declared, and Eva got a Post Graduate seat in Lucknow, her alma mater. Of them all, only Eva and Saurav cleared the exams. Undeniably, the events of the few months before the exams did have an impact on their studies. Eva counted herself lucky she was still able to clear her exams with a good rank. After the counselling was over, she was busy with the admission process in Lucknow. Then she had gone home to spend some time at home before joining the post-graduation course. Almost everyone had left Delhi except Rahul who stayed back to prepare again. The others had all returned to their respective hometowns to work. In a way, everything that had happened had had some influence on their decisions. No one really wanted to remain in Delhi. The memories were too fresh. Every place was a constant reminder of the tragedy of losing their friend. Nisha too had left to join a mission hospital in a small town in UP. She said she couldn't bear to stay in Delhi and working in a small place would give her time to heal. Gradually, after joining her post graduate studies, Eva had been caught up in her work. She slowly lost touch with everyone. Nisha had said she would call Eva once she settled down, but she never did. So gradually everyone grew apart, busy with their own lives, blissfully unaware that the events of the past will have a bearing on the future, that the past will repeat itself.

CHAPTER 18

When Eva opened her eyes, it was already seven-thirty. Ban had just come in from a swim in the hotel's swimming pool. A fitness freak, he compensated his morning runs by swimming in the hotel pool.

"Ah! Sleeping Beauty's awake," he teased.

"I got up at six-thirty, but I didn't want to disturb you, so I showered and went out for a swim."

"Yes," replied Eva, "I couldn't sleep for a long time. I kept thinking of Nisha. Poor girl. Life was so hard for her, she had no one to turn to. And to give up her baby, it must have broken her inside."

"Ban, what do we do now? I mean if we find her child will Dinesh accept her? Who will be responsible for her?"

"Eva, I think Nisha wants us to find her daughter and take her to Debojit's parents. It's a bit difficult I must say. Because we don't know their address and if they are even still alive, but don't worry. God will guide us in this. We will make sure Nisha's last wish is fulfilled."

So, they both got dressed and went downstairs for breakfast. As they were eating, Eva called home and spoke with her daughters. Amanda had exciting news, "Mummy we got a dog. I mean a small puppy came

Printed in Great Britain
by Amazon

65645139R00069

home yesterday, and we gave it milk and Deng gave it a bath. It just wouldn't leave so we made a bed for it in the storeroom. Mummy can we keep it please?" Eva smiled and handed over the phone to Ban.

She could hear cries of "Please Papa." Eventually Ban put the phone against his chest and asked her, "What do you say?"

Eva could see that Ban too wanted to keep the puppy. He loved animals and so did she. She nodded. Ban then spoke to his sister Wanda, "Please take the puppy to the vet first, and start the vaccinations."

Even from where she sat Eva could hear whoops of joy coming over the phone. She took the phone and heard cries of joy. "Thank you, Mummy." Both girls chirped.

Eva's spirits lifted after talking to her daughters and she was determined to make sure Nisha's daughter is happy too.

By ten-thirty, Eva could not wait any longer. She was anxious and tense as to how Dinesh would react when he came to know of Nisha's past. It was a huge thing to know that your spouse had kept such a huge secret all the years together. Eva was worried. Even during the drive to Saket, Eva couldn't help but think about what Dinesh's reaction would be. And she could see Ban was worried too as he was quiet throughout the journey.

When they reached the café, the found Dinesh already waiting for them. He gave them a sheepish grin. "To tell you the truth, I couldn't sleep the whole night. I felt morning couldn't come soon enough. I couldn't wait any longer to know what Nisha had to say. Her last words."

On hearing this, Eva was at a loss of words. She silently handed him the letter. Dinesh took it, a puzzled look on his face. "You want me to read the letter?" he asked. Eva nodded. "I think you should read it for yourself. It's something Nisha should have told you herself long ago, but she lacked the courage. I think she would want you to read this yourself."

In order to give Dinesh some semblance of privacy as he read the letter, Eva and Ban went up to the counter to order some coffee for the three of them. When they returned to the table, they found Dinesh staring off in the distance, his face ashen, tears pouring down his cheeks. When he saw them, something seemed to break inside him, he had the look of a man defeated.

"Why?" he sobbed. "In all these years of our marriage she never confided in me. There was never a moment she let me know she was unhappy. Why did she live a life of pretence with me? I loved her so much. I would never have taken it against her. I would have loved her all the same. After all it was all in the past, before she even knew me. And none of it was her fault. It was just that at the time the circumstances were so different. Life had been so hard for her. I would have adopted her daughter if only she had told me. I would have raised her as my own."

"I think she was scared Dinesh." Eva replied. "I think she was scared of losing you and Meera too. Whatever happened had had a big impact on her psyche. The guilt of her past against the happiness of her present drove her to take her own life. She kept it all bottled up inside her, never telling a soul. If only she had confided in someone, you or me or anyone close to her, the outcome might have been different."

"What should I do now, Eva? What do I tell Meera? And how do I even tell her that her mother had a secret life before, that she already had a daughter?"

Ban looked at Dinesh, his eyes understanding the pain the other was going through. "Let us try to find the girl first. Eva and I will go to Allahabad as soon as we get reservations and talk to the old nurse's daughter. We will find out where the girl is now, and we will let you know."

"No," said Dinesh. "I'll come with you. After all this I want to make sure Nisha's daughter is alright. Even if I couldn't be there for her when she was alive, the least I can do is help find her daughter."

"But what about Debojit's parents Ban? Do we try to contact them now?" asked Eva.

"I think we should wait," said Ban. "Let's go to Allahabad first and then see what to do from there. When we find out where the girl is then we can contact them."

Dinesh still looked lost and unhappy, and Eva's heart went out for him. The pain and misery in his eyes were obvious. Losing his wife like that and then finding out she had kept such a secret from him was taking its toll. However, he controlled his emotions. "I'll make reservations for us. When do you all want to leave?" They all agreed it would be best to go as soon as they got confirmed reservations by train, as it was only an overnight journey from Delhi. Eva told Dinesh that she and Ban will make arrangements for the hotel as soon as the tickets were confirmed.

So, after finalising all the plans, they parted ways.

CHAPTER 19

Eva and Ban arrived at New Delhi Railway Station at around eight-thirty in the evening. The previous day after they had left Dinesh in the café, they had gone on to Sarojini Nagar to browse through the market there. They had bought a few knick knacks for the girls, but mainly the busy market, the colourful stalls and the typical chaos of shoppers jostling each other and hawkers shouting at the top of their lungs had served to take their minds off what had happened. Sarojini Market was huge, and they wandered around, bargaining for the few things they bought even though the prices were cheap compared to Shillong. But it was a pleasant change, allowing them to forget all the problems for a while.

By the time they had gotten back to the hotel, Dinesh had called saying he had made reservations by the Prayag Raj Express for the next day at 9:20 pm. Eva had then made hotel reservations for the three of them at The Allahabad Residency which was said to be located at the centre of the city according to the website.

So here they were, both of them in Platform 16 of the New Delhi Station, waiting for Dinesh. It had been years since Eva had travelled by train and being in the station brought back memories of the old days in college when she had travelled by train. During their MBBS days, they

preferred to travel by AC coaches but then reservations were not always easy to get so many a times Eva and other North-eastern students had travelled home by Sleeper Class too. The railways have improved a lot since then but Ban, having never been in the chaos and dirt of a north Indian railway station, was horrified.

Seeing his face, Eva laughed. "Wait till we get on the train."

"Is it really that bad, Eva?" he asked.

"No dear. We are travelling by one of the best trains around." She assured him.

Soon Dinesh arrived and they greeted one another like old friends, the tragedy of Nisha's death had brought them close. Dinesh, on his part seemed quite relieved to have someone who didn't judge him for what had happened. And more important, who knew his wife and didn't pass judgement on her actions. Though the circumstances were somewhat surreal, he knew Eva shared a deep bond with Nisha and somehow having her and her husband along on this journey to find Nisha's daughter seemed somewhat appropriate. And again, after getting to know them, Dinesh found he liked both Eva and Ban. They gave him the space to grieve his recent loss yet made him feel at home and cared for. He felt genuine friendship and concern when he was with them. Perhaps this was what gave him the strength to go begin this journey, painful though it was for him, though he seldom admitted this, even to himself. But he wanted to honour Nisha's last wish, and he was grateful he had friends like Eva and Ban to help him through these difficult times.

The three of them got on the train. Their tickets were 2 Tier AC, and it was a comfortable journey. Once the train started moving, Eva unpacked their dinner, a KFC bucket and burgers which Ban had got on their way to the station. Somehow being on the train and doing something so mundane as eating KFC helped take their minds off the actual reason for their trip. They chatted about the past, recalling anecdotes from Nisha's life and it made her come alive in their memories and strangely this brought comfort to both Dinesh as well as Eva.

CHAPTER 20

The train arrived on time in Allahabad at 7 am. Eva woke up around six-thirty in the morning to find Ban and Dinesh already chatting over cups of hot milky tea. Dinesh went and got another cup for her from a vendor standing in the cramped passage near the coach doors. Eva took a sip and savoured the strong milk *chai*. The tea in north India is in a class of its own. It was hot, thick, aromatic and delicious. She missed the tea most from her college days. Back in Shillong, tea was different, made in British style with the milk and sugar added separately to the cup. It was a delicate, genteel flavour, usually served in bone china cups and accompanied by an assortment of cakes or sandwiches if you were visiting someone's home or in less fancy china mugs at home or in the numerous tea shops across Shillong. In north India, tea was a lifeline, people drank it in the bitter winter cold as well as the sweltering summer's heat. It bonded people together with crowds around small makeshift teashops ever present in front of any big building. She looked at Ban and gave a wry grin. "See, this is what I told you about. This is how tea should be made. Strong and thick enough to warm the cockles of the heart." He laughed and told Dinesh, "Eva loves her tea, and she insists we make it at home this way."

"You and Meera should visit us, Dinesh, I guarantee you tea is what you will miss most." At that time Eva didn't realise that her words were almost prophetic. Soon the train stopped at Platform 1 of the Alahabad Junction. They got down from the train and made their way out of the station. Eva had asked the hotel to arrange for a pickup and the scanned the crowds for someone with a placard bearing her name. They spotted the man and were led to a waiting cab and were soon whisked away from the station towards their hotel.

Allahabad was quite different after the bustling metropolitan atmosphere of Delhi. Here, the city gave a relaxed vibe, and having been one of the important centres of the British Raj, there were many structures and buildings left from that era. This gave the city a sense of timelessness, of a seamless coexistence of the modern city with the charm of a bygone era. As they drove in the early morning, the sun was coming up and the city seemed to slowly awaken from its slumber. Eva felt a serenity, a sense of unhurried calm. They soon reached their hotel. It was in the centre of the city, in a place called Civil Lines. Although Eva had seen pictures of the hotel online when she made the bookings, she was blown away when they arrived at the hotel. Set in a huge expanse of well-manicured lawns, the hotel resembled a well-kept British bungalow. It was as if it had stood there unaffected by the passage of time. The lobby had high backed chairs and had the feel of someone's opulent study or den. After the formalities of registration were complete, they were taken to their rooms. They had adjoining rooms with Dinesh, and here in the hotel it seemed unbelievable that they were in the middle of a big crowded Indian city.

They freshened up after the journey and soon went for breakfast. When they enquired at the lobby, they were directed towards a quaint restaurant on the lawn where breakfast was served. As they ate, they talked about the best way to approach Dr Singh, Mrs Lin's daughter.

"Should we call her first?" asked Dinesh, "Or should we just go to her clinic?"

"It's a difficult situation," said Ban. "Poor lady will be shocked out of her wits to see three complete strangers barging into her clinic asking about a baby her mother had adopted. We need to be discreet. Present the matter with some finesse. What do you say, Eva?"

"Yes," she agreed. "But we do not have another option either. We do not know her at all, and such matters cannot be discussed over the telephone. I think we should go to her clinic, introduce ourselves, and ask her to meet us for coffee when she's free at the earliest. We can tell her it's a something related to Nisha and her mother. And for all we know, her mother might still be living here in Allahabad, meaning Nisha's daughter might be here as well."

"If that's the case it would simplify things for us, wouldn't it, Ban?" asked Dinesh.

"Let's not get ahead of ourselves here," said Ban. "We should go and talk to the doctor first and see. But I think Eva's idea is good. We'll not disturb her clinic schedule. We can ask her to meet us when she's free."

That decided, they finished their breakfast. A hearty fare of *alu parathas* and curd, with omelettes on the side as well as hot steaming cups of *chai*.

They agreed to go to the clinic at 12 noon since Eva said that the doctor might be taking her rounds in the hospital in the morning. So, Eva went to her room to call her daughters while Ban and Dinesh went out for a stroll in the streets.

CHAPTER 21

They reached the clinic at 12 noon. In her letter Nisha had written the address as Ladies' Clinic, Tagore Town, Allahabad. So, Dinesh had enquired at the hotel reception on how to get there. Here they soon learned that the old-world charm of Allahabad extended to its transport system as well. The city did not have a public transport system in the form of buses or cabs but relied on cycle rickshaws and a peculiar kind of three wheelers called *tempos*, which are actually bigger that your normal autorickshaw and carried a full load of passengers. In the end they had asked the hotel to arrange for a car for hire for the duration of their stay.

Driving through the city in the midday traffic was overwhelming to say the least. The roads were crowded with interstate buses and cars, with cycle rickshaws and two wheelers jostling for space. On top of that, there were people travelling by bicycles along the side of the road. It seemed to Eva it was a miracle to be able to drive without hitting anyone. The illusion of peace and tranquility of the morning drive had been shattered and in its place was a cacophony of horns and full-blown chaos.

At the clinic, Eva had introduced herself at the reception and said that she had come on a personal matter. They had been told that the doctor would be in

after an hour, so they settled down to wait. Eva's mind went back to the conversation she had with her daughters on the phone that morning. Both girls sounded happy, though they asked her when she was coming home. Eva had no specific answer so she just told them they will be home soon. But as she sat there waiting, she felt close to tears. She missed her daughters badly, she missed her home, her work. She missed the peaceful atmosphere of Shillong, where the pollution was lesser, and the air was clear and crisp. And as the monsoon gave way to autumn, Shillong usually had clear blue skies and bright sunlight. And at that moment she felt as if she was a thousand miles away from home, in a strange place, under surreal circumstances. She was lost in her thoughts when the doctor walked in.

After a few minutes the receptionist beckoned them inside. They entered the chamber and introduced themselves to Dr Singh. Dinesh introduced himself as Nisha's husband and said they had come about the child Dr Singh's mother had adopted.

"I had read about the suicide in the papers," she replied. "Wondered what had happened and since Nisha had decided not to keep in touch, I couldn't contact anyone."

"You see, Nisha had left a letter in my name," said Eva. "She had written about how wonderful you and your mother had been to her. How you had helped her, and most importantly how your mother had taken in her baby when Nisha had lost all hope. But she had also written that she wanted to right all her wrongs and she wanted her daughter to meet Debojit's parents."

"Dr Singh, I realise this puts you in an awkward position. You might be feeling that we have come to take away the child from your mother after she has raised her for so long." said Dinesh.

"Call me Margaret. And no, it's a relief actually. Don't get me wrong. We all love Trisha. That's the name my mother gave her. After her retirement my mum went back to Meghalaya with Trisha, back to our village." Dr Margaret went on to tell them how her mother Mrs Dalin, or Mrs Lin as Nisha called her, had loved Trisha like her own. She always said that she felt the child was a gift God had given her to be with her in her old age, as her own daughter Dr Margaret had gotten married and settled far away from her hometown. And Trisha returned the love in full measure. She was a happy child with a quick intellect and very pretty.

Margaret looked at Eva and Ban, "Mummy passed away last year, so Trisha has been living with with my aunt and her children back home. They stay in a small village near Laitlyngkot. Everyone back home loves Trisha, but we are in a kind of dilemma. Sometimes we feel maybe she should know her real family. She loved Mummy so much and after her death, the poor child seemed a bit lost."

Eva was stunned to hear this. After all this journey, Nisha's daughter was so close to home. Perhaps that was why Nisha had asked Eva to look for her (Nisha's) daughter and unite her with Debojit's parents.

Eva looked at Ban and Dinesh and spoke. "Dr Margaret, I hope it would be possible for us to go and meet Trisha. Does she know the truth about her parents?"

"Not fully. My mother told her that her parents are dead. She even writes Lyngdoh as her surname. I can give you the address if you want to meet her. I'll tell my aunt, so she'll be expecting you."

"Thank you so much. We really can't thank you enough," said Dinesh. "But we need to discuss and make plans to go there. We'll let you know as soon as we can."

So, they all shook hands with the doctor and took their leave.

CHAPTER 22

"So, what do we do next?" asked Dinesh. All three of them had gathered in Dinesh's room to discuss the latest turn of events. Eva was shocked by the knowledge that all these years Nisha's daughter had been living so close to her home. She thought that if only Nisha had confided in her, trusted her, things might have been very different. Dinesh's words broke into her thoughts.

"I think we should go and meet her first. Though I don't know how much we should tell her and if she will be able to understand. Poor child, she is so young and with such a tragic story," she replied, a thoughtful look on her face.

"But she deserves to know the truth, don't you think?" asked Dinesh. "It's time this whole sad story is given closure. And Nisha wanted us to do that, to take her daughter back to Debojit's parents."

"Yes, Dinesh. You're right. I think we should go and meet Trisha. In the meantime, we can try to find Debojit's parents. I don't even know if they're still alive." There was worry in Eva's voice.

It was Dinesh who spoke now. "Eva, Ban, you have been a tremendous help for me. I could have never survived the shock of Nisha's suicide if it hadn't been

for both of you. But being by my side and helping me find her daughter has helped me come to terms with my grief. But I think before we proceed further, I should go home and talk to Meera. She is only eight years old, and if we suddenly introduce her to Trisha, she wouldn't understand. I think I should go to Nainital and talk to her and then bring her along with us. Maybe you can go ahead to Shillong and wait for me there. When I come along with Meera, we can all go and meet Trisha. I have a feeling this is what my wife would have wanted. For both her daughters to get to know each other."

On hearing this, Eva's respect for Dinesh could only increase. He loved his wife so much, that even after she kept such a huge part of her life from him, lying about her past, he forgave her and was even willing to look for her daughter. Nisha's last wishes were foremost in his mind, and he wanted to keep them to the very end.

"How many days do you need to go to Nainital, Dinesh?" asked Ban. "If it's only for a few days we can all travel to Delhi, and we can wait for you there, and then travel to Shillong together."

"It would take three days for me to come back to Delhi. We'll reach Delhi on Saturday morning. I'll go on to Nainital the same day and I'll be back by Monday."

"So, we can get tickets to Guwahati for Tuesday," said Ban. "Then we'll all go home. You and Meera can stay with us."

At this Dinesh protested saying he will book a hotel; he didn't want to trouble them.

Eva looked at him and said, “If Nisha had still been here and you all visited Shillong, you would be staying at my place. Do you think she’ll ever forgive me from beyond the grave if I made you stay in a hotel?”

Dinesh gave a sheepish smile. “I think we’ve had enough talk. Suddenly I’m hungry. Since we missed lunch, let’s go out and eat something. Might as well try some of the famous Allahabadi cuisine.” Ban gave Eva a smile. Dinesh had come a long way from the broken man they had first met in Delhi. He seemed more at peace. Maybe carrying out Nisha’s last wishes helped him come to terms with what had happened. Anyway, it was a good sign. Since he would have to be there for Meera, be her rock for the times to come.

CHAPTER 23

"Wow, the food here is unbelievable." Ban declared with his mouth full. They were sitting in a restaurant in Civil Lines, a posh area of Allahabad. It was an old establishment but had been highly recommended by the hotel reception.

And they were not disappointed. They had ordered kebabs and tandoori chicken accompanied by *roomali* rotis. The aromas wafting in the restaurant whetted their appetites and when the food arrived it was wonderful. The flavour and taste of the kebabs impressed even Ban who considered himself a food critic. The tandoori chicken was moist and succulent, melt in your mouth, and the rotis lived upto their name, soft and fluffy. As they ate, they made plans on how to proceed on their journey, their quest to find Nisha's daughter.

"I think you should try to contact your old friends Eva," said Ban. "Maybe someone has Debojit's parents' address or better still a phone number."

"I don't really think anyone will have his parents' phone number after so long, but I think I have his address written in my old diary back home."

"But do you think they're still living in the same place?" asked Dinesh.

"I really don't know," replied Eva. "I think it was their own house, not rented so it's likely they will still be living there."

"I have Rahul and Saurav's phone numbers. I'll call them later tonight or tomorrow morning to find out more."

Actually, Eva had wanted to call Rahul and Saurav as well as John, Mami and Zuali as soon as she had read Nisha's letter, but she felt they should all talk to Dinesh first. It now directly involved him, and his daughter Meera and she didn't know how Dinesh would react. After all, what had happened had turned his life upside down. So, she had decided to wait. But now everything seems to be falling into place and Dinesh seemed to have accepted what had happened. So, she decided it was time to call her old friends and let them know what had happened.

They had finished their food and taste buds sated, they were lingering over coffee when Eva's phone rang. It was Dr Margaret. She called to ask them for coffee at her house. She said she lived just behind her clinic in Tagore Town and there were a few things she would like to talk about. Eva looked at Dinesh and Ban who were listening to her side of the conversation and said they would be there around 7pm.

CHAPTER 24

They reached Dr Margaret's house at 7 in the evening as agreed. The house was a posh modern two-storey, with lots of plants and greenery, suggesting a love for gardening. Dr Margaret was waiting for them, and she warmly welcomed them inside. She said she hardly had visitors from Shillong and although the circumstances were a bit strange, she felt a closeness to them, a kind of kinship. Over coffee and snacks she told them about how her mother took Nisha under her wing. After she learned of what had happened in Delhi, she felt sorry for Nisha. Dr Margaret said that her mother was a kind and gentle soul who could never see anyone suffering. So, she offered to take the baby and raise her.

"Anyway, Mummy always lamented the fact that since I got married and settled here, there would be no one to care for her in her old age. So, raising Nisha's baby made perfect sense. And Mummy always wanted to go back home. She said she wanted to die in her own village."

"Is Trisha happy there?" asked Dinesh.

"Oh, yes," she replied. "Whenever I visited, she was always happy. In fact, she had adapted perfectly to life over there, no one would know she is not a Khasi. And Mummy loved Trisha. Whenever she has holidays,

Mummy used to take her to Shillong for shopping, or to visit relatives. But then my mother was diagnosed with oesophageal cancer, and she expired six months later. Before she died, she made me promise to look after Trisha. Trisha was with her until the very end. Poor kid seemed so lost without Mummy."

"You've been a blessing for us, Dr Margaret," said Eva. "We had no idea how to proceed to carry out Nisha's wish. Your address was the only link we had."

"In a way, I'm glad you all came here, despite the tragic circumstances. You see, I had been planning to bring Trisha here with me. But I didn't want to uproot her from there. She hardly knows me. She is staying with my aunt for now, but it isn't permanent."

"That's what," said Eva. "As Nisha wanted, we will try to unite her with Debojit's parents."

"And if that does not work out, I'm ready to adopt her." Dinesh said with a quiet determination. Again, Eva marvelled at Dinesh's strength and character, at what a good-hearted and unique person he is. And then it struck Eva that Trisha does not know of the circumstances of her birth. She had been told that her parents were dead, which is in a way true, but Eva was worried how she would react when she learned that her mother had been alive all these years, and of the tragedies involving first her father and then her mother.

"Dr Margaret, as you said, Trisha does not know the truth about her parents. It would be very hard on an 11-year-old to learn the truth and then process it."

"Eva, if I might suggest something," said Dr Margaret. "It would be better if you contact the grandparents first and if possible, take them with you when you go and see Trisha. As a child she would not be able to fully understand the circumstances, the happenings of the past. But it will surely help if her grandparents are there. It would make her feel loved and wanted. She will slowly accept and come to terms with the past as she grows up, but right now, she needs love and a family."

"You're right," replied Eva. "We had not thought of this. Actually, we had not given much thought on how to approach Trisha, but this is an excellent idea. This way would make her feel better and lessen the hurt of the past. As a child she might not be able to understand most of it, but it would break her hear that her mother had abandoned her. Having her grandparents there would take away the pain to a certain extent."

They stayed and chatted about Shillong for some more time. Before they left, Dr Margaret gave them her aunt's phone number and address in Meghalaya. Sha also told them to call her and let her know what happens.

CHAPTER 25

Eva woke up from a deep slumber. She opened her eyes and found Ban staring at her. "What time is it?" "It's eleven thirty," he replied. It was Saturday morning. They had arrived by train from Allahabad at 6:30 am and had said goodbye to Dinesh at the station. He left to continue on to Nainital while they waited in Delhi. Eva and Ban had then gone to their hotel in New Friends' Colony, the same one they had stayed earlier. It felt a bit like coming home. They had then gone straight to bed to get a few hours' sleep. After everything that had happened, they felt a need to recharge. This trip had been emotionally exhausting and had taken quite a toll on them. Now for the next two days while they waited for Dinesh, they planned to relax and rest.

"How about we order some coffee and snacks from room service?" said Ban. "My stomach is rumbling."

Eva smiled. She suddenly realised she was ravenous too. "Let's get some club sandwiches and fries. Then we can have a late lunch. And what will we do today, honey?"

"Actually, I was planning to go and meet some wholesalers for some winter stock for the shops. Do you want to come with me, or would you rather rest here?"

"No, you go ahead," said Eva. "I'd like to stay here if you don't mind."

They showered and dressed and soon the food arrived. After they ate, Eva called home. Both the girls were thrilled that they would be back home by Tuesday. Eva too was happy to be going back home. She missed her daughters sorely and in just another three days she would be home. But of course, there were endless demands for presents. She spoke to Wanda, Ban's sister and told her they would be bringing two guests along. She asked her to tell Deng, their helper, to prepare the guest room for Dinesh. In the meantime, Clarissa can move in with Amanda and Meera can sleep in her room. The girls were excited to hear that she was bring some guests home and that one of them is a little girl. She was smiling when she hung up the phone. How she missed her daughters.

Ban soon left for his work, and Eva called Saurav, who is now a surgeon with his own practice in Guwahati. He was surprised to hear from her, and when she told him the reason for her call, he remained silent for a long time. Then he replied, "Eva, I'm shocked beyond words by this news. I never imagined that the past would come to haunt us like this. Poor Nisha. Life was so cruel to her. But you're right. We should bring her daughter to Debojit's parents. Maybe Nisha's soul will find peace in the afterlife. Uncle and Aunty are still living here in Guwahati. Rahul and I used to visit them sometimes, but I don't have their phone number."

"No," Eva replied. "I don't think this can be discussed over the phone anyway. It will be a shock for them too. We are flying to Guwahati on Tuesday. Maybe you can

take us to their house. Nisha's husband and daughter are coming with us."

"Oh, yes. Absolutely. I'll call Rahul too. And John and Zuali have settled in Guwahati too. We can all go together and meet Uncle and Aunty. Both of them are still quite healthy. I'm sure once the initial shock wears off, they would be happy to have Debojit's daughter with them."

"Let's not get ahead of ourselves," said Eva. Saurav was still the same. Always the optimist. Anyway, she thanked him and disconnected the call. She then called Mami in Aizawl and told her about the turn of events. Mami was shocked too, and the two of them talked about the past and how Nisha had ruined her life by not confiding in any of them. Maybe if she had done so, life would have taken a different turn. Maybe she would still be alive.

The phone calls left Eva drained. She felt a deep sense of sadness for Nisha, whose life had ended so tragically. But she reminded herself to stay strong. She had to complete the task her friend had entrusted her with. Nisha's last wish. For her daughter to be united with Debojit's parents. This strangely gave her some comfort and the grit to go ahead until she found Nisha's daughter.

CHAPTER 26

Tuesday morning dawned bright and brilliant. It was a beautiful day. Eva sat in the hotel lounge waiting for their car to take them to the airport. Dinesh and Meera had arrived on Monday evening and had stayed at the same hotel with Eva and Ban. Meera was a cute bubbly little girl who was the spitting image of Nisha. The tragic loss of her mother was reflected in her eyes, but with the resilience of children she seemed to somehow cope with it. And of course, the trip to Shillong made her extremely excited. The night before Dinesh had introduced Eva as "Mummy's best friend" and after that with a childlike innocence she had warmed up to Eva, maybe it made her feel closer to her mother. Just once she had asked if her mother was in heaven now, to which Eva had hugged her and told her yes, Nisha is watching over them from heaven.

Eva watched Ban telling Meera about their own daughters, Amanda and Clarissa.

"And you and your Papa will stay in our house, and you will get to play with them. And we'll go out for picnics too."

Meera squealed with delight. "And you will get to meet your sister Trisha." said Dinesh.

"Oh yes. Can she come back with us, Papa?" Meera asked.

"Let's see when we get there my dear," replied Dinesh.

Eva listened to this and smiled. Dinesh had told Meera that they were going to Shillong to meet her sister Trisha, who was staying with some relatives there. He told her that Trisha is Mummy's daughter before she started her life with them. It was not the whole truth, but it was sufficient to assuage the eight-year-old Meera's curiosity. Now the child felt like it was a wonderful adventure to go to Shillong and meet new friends and a sister. Eva thought that Dinesh had handled the whole situation well. He had told Meera that her mother Nisha had had a daughter, Trisha, before they had gotten married. But that the child's father had died so Nisha had left her daughter with some relatives. And now they were going to meet Trisha and her grandparents.

Soon the car came, and they were off to the airport. Eva sat with Meera and Dinesh in the back of the car while Ban sat in front. Maybe it was Meera's excitement affecting them, but everyone seemed to be in a joyful, excited mood. The tragic mood, the sadness that had enveloped them seem to have lifted and there was an air of hope and excitement for the future.

CHAPTER 27

Eva stood just outside the arrivals terminal at Guwahati airport and scanned the crowd for Saurav. As she stood there amidst the din of taxi drivers calling out for passengers to Shillong and others trying to pick up passengers for Guwahati, she felt a sense of homecoming. Amidst the din she could catch a word or two of Khasi, her mother tongue, as taxis from Shillong regularly brought passengers down to the airport and picked up others on the way back. She also felt relieved to be back after such an emotionally charged trip. Looking over at the others, she saw her own feelings reflected in her husband's face; but as for Dinesh, his face was a mixture of emotions. It was a mixture of trepidation as well as a haunting sadness that seemed to be emanating deep from within his soul. Meera of course, was full of excitement.

"Eva, here, this way," she heard a familiar voice and there was Saurav towering over them. And behind him were John and Zuali.

Eva introduced everyone and hugged Zuali. Both of them couldn't hold back the tears as they stood there in the crowded airport. It felt as if the years had melted away and they were back at Delhi airport saying their final goodbyes to Debojit. They composed themselves and then Eva asked where they were to go now.

"We will all go to John and Zuali's first so you all can freshen up," replied Saurav. "Rahul will meet us there."

John and Zuali lived in a nice quiet neighbourhood in the city. They had a 7-year-old son, but he was at his school, so the house was quiet. There Eva introduced Dinesh and Meera. By that time, Rahul had also arrived, and they all listened as Dinesh told of the sad and harrowing event of his wife's suicide. He then told them of how he had found the letter addressed to Eva. Never did he imagine the contents of the letter would turn out to be so hear wrenching. Everyone had tears in their eyes when he told them about Trisha, the daughter Nisha had had to abandon as a baby. But with a firm resolve and a quiet determination in his voice he told them that he wanted to make sure that Nisha's last wishes were fulfilled. He would make sure Trisha would be united with her grandparents.

Everyone sat in shocked silence. Zuali was weeping inconsolably, and Eva had her arm around her friend.

"Why didn't Nisha ever say anything to anyone of us?" said Zuali.

"We would have definitely tried to come up with a solution and help her. She kept such a huge secret bottled inside her which ultimately cost her her life."

Everyone was lost in their own thoughts. It seemed that the events of the past have caught up with them. Their minds went back to the day Debojit committed suicide and the events that unfolded thereafter. It seemed like just a while back they had said their final goodbyes to Debojit. But the years had passed by and they never

for once imagined that the events of the past would lead to another suicide amongst them. That Nisha would be in such a desperate situation, alone and pregnant with no one to turn to that ultimately, she had to give up her baby. And the guilt and remorse of her actions would haunt her throughout her life and ultimately cause her to take her own life.

Saurav spoke up. "Eva, I had called up Uncle last night. I didn't tell him anything. I just said that you were coming to Guwahati and would like to see them. It just didn't seem right if we all just dropped in on them with such momentous news."

"You're right Saurav," said Eva. "I just hadn't thought of that. I really don't know how to tell them about all this. At first, I had thought we should go and meet Trisha first and then bring her along with us. But then that would be too much of a shock."

"So, I thought we should go meet them first and tell them about what had happened and that they have a granddaughter, their son's own flesh and blood. Then if they are up to it, we can all go to Shillong and meet Trisha."

Dinesh then told them, "I have been thinking about this. In case Debojit's parents don't want to take Trisha, I would be happy to adopt her. She is Meera's sister after all and Nisha loved her so much, she gave up her life for her. I think this would bring her peace."

Eva's respect for Dinesh grew more as she heard these words. She wondered how many men would be willing to adopt their wife's illegitimate daughter, especially

after such a tragedy. That Dinesh was willing to do so spoke volumes of what a wonderful human being he was. He loved his wife and forgave her and was ready to do anything which would have made her happy. Eva wondered if Nisha had come clean to Dinesh maybe she would still be alive, and Dinesh could have adopted Trisha. But as fate would have it, that was an alternate reality that never happened, and Eva realised that it was foolish to dwell on the might-have-beens.

CHAPTER 28

As the car drew up in front of Debojit's parents house, Eva felt a sense of trepidation. What if they did not want to see Trisha? Was it even fair to open the old wounds of Debojit's suicide? After all time is a great healer and they must have accepted their son's death. Would it only cause them more sadness in their old age to relive the past? She looked at Ban and he gave her hand a reassuring squeeze. Dinesh sat in front lost in his thoughts and Meera sat next to Eva. Perhaps she could sense the seriousness of the situation and sat quietly looking at Dinesh's phone.

But all the misgivings disappeared as soon as she saw Debojit's parents come out of the house. They must've heard the cars pull up. Aunty hugged Eva and Zuali and welcomed everyone. Their home was neat and had a loving homely feeling which put everyone at ease.

Eva introduced Ban to them. "This is my husband, Bantei."

Aunty hugged him and asked Eva how many children they have. Ban produced a picture from his wallet and told them about the girls. Eva then introduced Dinesh and Meera as Nisha's husband and daughter. Aunty smiled at them and then asked Dinesh why Nisha hadn't

come along. Dinesh looked at Eva for an answer, but Meera was quicker. "My Mummy's in heaven."

The silence that followed was deafening. It seemed to Eva that time froze at that moment. Then she heard Zuali sobbing and even she couldn't hold back her tears any longer. It was as if the floodgates opened. She told Debojit's parents the whole story from the beginning when she heard the news of Nisha's suicide. She and Aunty held each other and cried. They cried for Debojit, for Nisha, for somehow the past and the present had blended together and as they stood there, Eva finally felt a sense of closure, a sense of peace that had been missing from the time Debojit died. And Eva could see the same emotion in Aunty's eyes. That was when Eva realised that they had done the right thing coming here.

Aunty made tea for them and over cups of tea she asked Eva details of Trisha, her new-found granddaughter. The old couple looked radiant, as if they have received a gift of life. Eva showed them Nisha's letter after asking Dinesh's permission. The elderly couple took it and tears flowed as they read about how Nisha was so desperate, she had to give away her baby.

"If only she had called us," said Aunty. "Of course, we would have taken care of her. It is our son's child she was carrying. Even though they were not married, yet Debojit had planned to bring her home before he took his own life. But God has his own plans. Nisha was lucky to have found a husband like Dinesh and she had a wonderful daughter, Meera."

"Anyway, maybe it's God's will that we find our granddaughter, a beacon of hope in our old age. It is as

though my son has been given back to us." Both of them beamed.

And just like that everyone's mood lifted. It was as if the storm of melancholy, dread and sadness that had stifled the room had suddenly vanished and in its place was happiness and hope. Hope that finally all the sadness and grief that had begun 12 years ago, with a loss of two precious lives, has given way to joy. It was as if it was meant to be that Debojit and Nisha's daughter would be a source of love and hope for his parents, the same love and hope that they had lost when death had cruelly snatched away their son at such a young age.

CHAPTER 29

Eva sat at the window of their hired Innova for the journey home. It was early November, but the hills were still a rich verdant green from the last monsoon. Eva realised how much she missed these green forests of Meghalaya. The lush greenery along the highway from Guwahati always instilled in her a sense of tranquillity especially during her college days, when she returned home for the summer breaks. After the sun scorched plains of North India, the green rolling hills, the splashing streams and the sudden rains or light drizzles seemed to envelop the senses in a cosy cocoon. She suddenly realised she had been away for 10 days; but it seemed as though an eternity had passed. After that fateful message on her phone informing her of Nisha's death, it had seemed as if the past and the present had somehow merged. The journey to Delhi had led them on a surreal quest to find Nisha's daughter; and here they were now on the way to Shillong, hopefully on the last leg of the task Nisha had entrusted her from beyond the grave.

She felt her husband give her shoulder a reassuring squeeze. He sat in the back seat with Dinesh and Meera, whereas Eva sat in the middle with Aunty. Uncle occupied the front passenger seat. His excitement knew no bounds. He had spent his college days in Shillong, and now going back with the prospect of meeting his newly found

granddaughter, it was as if Santa Claus had come bearing gifts in November.

The night before they had been in unsure if Uncle and Aunty should come along. Maybe it would be better if Eva, Ban, Dinesh and Meera went and met Trisha first and then bring her down to Guwahati. But Aunty had ruled over such arguments saying the poor girl had spent long enough believing she's an orphan. She has her own family, her own grandparents, willing to take her and give her the love she deserved.

"Eva, what are your plans when we reach Shillong?" Aunty asked.

"Do we go straight to this place where Trisha lives?"

"No, Aunty. We will go home first. By the time we reach Shillong it will be late afternoon. I think it would be better if we set out in the morning as Laitlyngkot is a little more than an hour's drive from Shillong. You all can stay the night at our house."

This statement was met with protests from both Dinesh and Aunty. Both were saying they don't want to impose on Eva and Ban.

"Both of you have gone out of your way to help me deal with this, Eva. I don't want to be a burden. Meera and I can put up in a hotel or guest house. I had done a bit of checking online."

"No, it is no burden at all. I would love to have you all stay in our house." Ban chimed in.

"I mean Nisha would never forgive Eva from beyond the grave if you all stayed at a hotel. I'm sure none of you would want my wife to be haunted forever." He joked.

So, it was all agreed that they would stay overnight at Eva's house and set out in the morning.

They reached Nongpoh, a small town situated around midway between Guwahati and Shillong. They all stopped for a quick cup of tea and snacks. Everyone welcomed the chance to stretch their legs. But Uncle stared aghast at the change.

"This new highway is superb, a far cry from the old road when we were in college, but I never dreamt Nongpoh had grown so much. Where are those thatched huts with wonderful Khasi food?" he lamented.

Eva laughed. "Uncle, only the thatched roofs have vanished. The food is very much the same."

Soon they were all tucking into an early lunch of rice with chicken and local bamboo shoot pickle accompanied by cups of piping hot black tea. After the meal, everyone felt refreshed and ready to continue the drive to Shillong.

CHAPTER 30

Eva woke up early the next morning slightly disoriented. She then realised that she was at home in her own bed and smiled. She felt completely relaxed to be home after the events of the past few days. Even though they still had to go and meet Trisha, she felt calm and relaxed. Just being home and seeing her daughters had taken away half her stress. The previous evening when they arrived home, her daughters had rushed out to meet them only to be surprised on seeing so many people. They had been shy at first but soon bonded with Meera after learning that her mother had been "Mummy's Best Friend." And on learning that they were going to meet Meera's sister the next day, their excitement knew no bounds and they had asked numerous questions until they fell asleep. Of course, there was no question about where Meera would sleep. The girls decided she should sleep with them. Uncle and Aunty had the guest room, and Eva made up a bed for Dinesh in Clarissa's room. She was worried that the room with its soft toys and girlish décor would bother Dinesh, but he didn't seem to mind.

When she went downstairs, she found Ban had started making breakfast with Deng their helper. The girls were crowded around Dinesh on the dining table. He was regaling them with takes from the hills Uttarakhand and

Amanda and Clarissa were listening to him with rapt attention. As soon as they saw her, they rushed forward for hugs. They turned to Meera and said, "Come over, hugs for you too." Eva was almost knocked over by the three of them.

She then went over to Ban to help serve the meal. To her astonishment, she found a stack of warm *alu-parathas* already made. Ban was just making omelettes and tea. He looked at her and grinned, "Good morning. Aunty got up at 6:30 and made this. She's such a dear. I love *parathas.*"

"I tried to stop her, but she wouldn't listen," said Deng.

"It's alright," replied Eva and winked at her husband, "It's such a delicious spread anyway."

Uncle and Aunty came in from the garden where they had been enjoying the crisp morning air, and everyone tucked heartily into their breakfast.

Eva looked around her with everyone chatting seemingly at ease with each other, and realised that given the circumstances, everything had turned out quite well. The whole journey they had undertaken with Dinesh had seemed to calm him and he had come to terms with his wife's death. The haunted look had left his eyes. He no longer seemed to be the broken man they had met in Delhi. And the change in environment seemed to have helped considerably. Seeing his daughter so full of life and vigour with her new friends seemed to give him an inner strength, a resilience to see through whatever this journey has in store. As for Uncle and Aunty, it seemed as if the

years had melted away. When she had first met them in Delhi, during those dark days after Debojit's death, they had looked lost, as though life had lost all meaning. Even though they had put up a brave front throughout all those days, it was obvious that their spirit was broken. When they had finally left Delhi with their son's body, it was as though they were questioning why fate had dealt them such a cruel hand. But seeing them now, there was a new spring in their step, their faces beaming with joy and hope and happiness.

But Eva's bubble was burst as soon as Amanda and Clarissa learnt that they were not included in the 'outing,' as they put it, to meet Meera's sister.

"Please Mummy, let us come too. We promise to be good," they both chimed.

"And we can show Meera the sights along the way. Please, please let us come."

Eva looked at the others. Dinesh was amused. Aunty gave a sheepish grin and said, "It would be a shame to leave them behind. Being with them is so wonderful."

So, it was decided that Ban and Eva and the three girls would go in Ban's car. And Uncle, Aunty and Dinesh would go in Eva's car with the driver.

CHAPTER 31

It was a glorious sunny November morning. This year winter had come early and there was a nip in the air. As they left the city, the highway was lined by blooming cherry trees whose beautiful pink blossoms made the drive ethereal. Shillong had an abundance of cherry trees, in and around the city, and each November the city was draped in a beautiful pink mantle of cherry blossoms drawing tourists from far and wide. Each autumn the city hosts numerous music festivals, food festivals, and the list goes on. But the Cherry Blossom Festival is a truly wonderful experience drawing people from all over the country. In November, Shillong shines in all its splendour. After the rain and fog of the monsoon, the crisp sunny days heralding the beginning of winter were a welcome respite. The brilliant sunshine and clear air also yielded a treat which was known to most locals but is usually met with disbelieving scepticism from others. In November, the Himalayas are visible from Shillong.

Eva smiled when she remembered the look of astonishment on Dinesh's face when she had told him the previous evening.

"You're kidding, right? We are so far away. How can it be possible to see the Himalayas from here?"

"Actually, the hills of Northeast are a part of the Himalayan range," Ban put in, a mischievous grin on his face, "So, in a way we are actually standing on the Himalayas."

"It's the Arunachal range visible from here, Mount Gorichen to be exact. Visible only in the month of November as the air is clear and the atmospheric conditions just right," said Eva. "I'll show you tomorrow."

So as the neared the Upper Shillong ridge, Eva asked Ban to stop. They got out of their car and waited for the others. As soon as Dinesh got there, his jaw dropped. Far away in the distant skyline, above the blue hills surrounding the city, the Himalayas were floating, like a vision in the clouds. It was a beautiful sight, and for Dinesh and Meera, totally unexpected. As they were from Nainital, seeing the Himalayas brought a sense of home.

"Oh, my God! It's true. I thought you were just pulling my leg, Eva."

Eva smiled at Dinesh. Meera was so excited, "Papa, can we see Naintal from here?"

"No darling," replied Dinesh. "This is a different stretch of the mountains. But it's beautiful."

Uncle and Aunty also marvelled at the sight. "Although I spent my college days here, I never actually saw the Himalayas, though I had heard about it. I always thought it was some kind of legend." Uncle beamed at them. His voice filled with nostalgia.

They continued their journey. Dinesh however, changed cars and sat with Meera and the girls in the back.

It was a little cramped, but Meera seemed to be feeling a little homesick and wanted her father with her.

As they drove on, Eva's mind wandered between the past and the present. She remembered Nisha, how they had spent their college days together, growing up together, removed from the comforts of home. They had been soulmates, and somehow Eva felt that after such upheavals in Nisha's life, it was somehow fitting that it was Eva who finally brought closure.

She dragged her mind back to the present and heard Dinesh and Meera marvelling over the landscape and scenery passing by. They had just reached the Headquarters of the Eastern Air Command and the scene was truly breath taking. Both sides of the road were lined with tall, majestic pines, each tree more than a century old. The brilliant blue skies, the green trees and the dappled sunlight along the road was postcard perfect. This particular stretch of the road never ceased to amaze visitors to Shillong. Soon they reached Mylliem where there were a lot of resorts, cafes as well as the well-loved local tea shops famous for smoked meats.

"There seems to be a huge crowd here," said Dinesh.

"This is a popular hangout," Ban replied. "People come here for a short drive and lunch. A short getaway from the traffic of Shillong. Some even cycle all the way here. Everyone comes for the food which is one of the best examples of Khasi home cooking. We'll stop here for tea."

Ban found a parking spot for the car. The other car also parked behind him. They all trooped into a local shop for tea and a selection of rice cakes.

As they sat sipped the hot black tea, their thoughts were on the journey ahead. Eva could see a sense of disquiet on Aunty's face. It was as though she equally welcomed and dreaded the task at hand.

She squeezed Aunty's hand. "Don't worry. Everything will be alright."

Aunty gave a grateful smile. "I hope Trisha accepts us. I'm so scared that she might not want to leave this place and come with us. I can't bear the thought of losing her. It would be like losing my son all over again."

"Don't worry. I called them last night. Mrs Lin's sister was very glad to hear that Trisha's grandparents are coming. I think she would have prepared Trisha to meet us all."

These words seemed to put the old couple's minds at ease. Dinesh, however, still had a look of unease.

CHAPTER 32

As they neared their destination, Eva's heart started to thump in her chest. She was swallowed by a sense of panic. Although she tried to keep a normal face for the others, inside she had a sense of déjà vu. Her mind went back to the night Debojit died when she and Nisha had gone to his hostel. She had that same feeling, dry-mouthed with fear and her heart thumping in her chest. Silently she prayed that everything would be alright. That whatever had gone wrong in Debojit's and Nisha's lives would be finally made right.

As they entered the picturesque village of Laitlyngkot, Eva called Mrs Lin's sister's number and asked for directions. The village was beautiful and very clean. The streets looked freshly swept and there was not a single piece of litter around. Almost every house whether big or small, had a small garden in front and flowers and orchids bloomed from pots in people's verandas and in some bigger houses, from terraces. Dinesh remarked that it certainly didn't look like a village, at least not his expectation of one. It looked more like a sub-urban colony, but a beautiful one. Eva couldn't agree more. Most of the villages around Shillong had beautiful modern houses usually in similar styles as the ones in the city, but often on huge plots of land. And most villages were meticulously clean. This,

combined with a natural love the Khasi people had of gardening, often turned each village into a quaint oasis of cleanliness and colour.

They soon found the house they were looking for. It was a bit further from the road accessed by a narrow lane with steps. A small boy was waiting for them beside the road. He showed them where to park their vehicles and skipped ahead of them towards the house. As they reached the gate, a woman came out to welcome them. She introduced herself as Kong Rilang, the youngest sister of Kong Dalin or Mrs Lin as Nisha had known her. Eva introduced herself and the others, telling Dinesh that Kong is a respectful term used for women in Khasi. As she spoke, she saw a face peeking from behind the curtains of one of the windows. She felt sure it was Trisha taking a peek at them.

They all entered the house and Eva then told Kong Rilang the whole story right from the beginning. About Nisha's suicide, her letter and about their journey from Delhi, to Allahabad, and finally now to this village in search of Nisha's daughter.

Kong Rilang looked at them. "I was surprised to hear from you," she said in halting English. She taught at a local primary school. "Ever since Kongheh, my sister, brought Trisha back with her when she retired, we were always told that she was an orphan, that her parents had died. Kongheh never told us the details, and since she loved Trisha so much, we never questioned anything. We accepted her as our own. And when my niece called up from Allahabad saying that you, Kong, had come looking for the child, and about the strange circumstances of her

birth, I really didn't know what to do. I felt that Kongheh had entrusted me with the responsibility of raising her daughter. For Trisha had really become a daughter to her."

She turned to Eva and said, "But I realised that as much as we love Trisha, it would be wrong to deprive her of her family. She loves us, I know. But she deserves to be with her grandparents. She deserves to know about her mother and half-sister. Most of all she deserves to know that she has a family."

As Kong Rilang was talking, tears were slowly falling down Aunty's face. "She is not an orphan. She is our child."

"I understand," replied Kong Rilang.

"For now, Trisha is happy to be here. She doesn't realise the complexities of her life. But when she gets older, she is bound to look for the truth regarding her parents."

Eva nodded vigorously, "And if she ever finds out the truth later on, it will hurt her deeply. Maybe that was the reason her mother's last wish was to bring Trisha back to her grandparents."

"Did you say anything to Trisha, Kong Rilang?" Eva asked. She was worried how a child might react to all this.

"I just explained to her that her Grandparents will be coming to meet her. I didn't say anything about her mother's death or anything else."

Eva shot a look of relief at her husband. Ban, and Dinesh who were sitting with the girls too looked relieved to hear this.

Aunty squeezed Eva's hand gently. Eva looked at her and understood the silent plea behind the old lady's tear-filled eyes.

"Kong Rilang, can we meet Trisha now?" Eva asked as she reassuringly squeezed Aunty's hand back.

"Of course. Let me go and get her. She's been excited since morning." Kong Rilang smiled as she got up from her chair. She seemed to be a soft-hearted loving person who instantly made Eva and the others feel at home. That was quite an achievement given the circumstances of their visit.

CHAPTER 33

As they waited for Trisha to make an appearance, it was as though time had stood still. Everyone sat with bated breath. Even the children seemed affected by the mood in the room and were quiet.

Eva looked around at Dinesh and Meera, at Uncle and Aunty, and she could read the tension in their eyes. They had come so far, and they were worried how things might go. Worried if what they were doing was right. After all it would mean uprooting Trisha from the only life she had known, from the love of people she had come to think as her own. All these emotions must have been reflected in her own eyes, for as her eyes locked with her husband's eyes across the room, he gave her a small smile.

"Don't worry, everything will be alright. This will bring peace to both Nisha and Debojit."

The door slowly opened, and a girl walked in followed by Kong Rilang. She was tall and lanky but was the spitting image of her mother Nisha. But she also inherited had father's curly hair, and with fair clear skin and long lashed eyes, it was obvious that she was going to be a beauty when she grew up.

"This is Trisha," Kong Rilang simply introduced the girl. "*Khun*, say hello to your Grandparents."

Aunty couldn't hold herself back. She got up and enveloped Trisha in a warm hug. Tears pouring down her face she said, "Darling, I'm your Grandma and this is your Grandpa. We are your Papa's Mummy and Papa."

Trisha looked lost and bewildered until Meera came forward. "You're my elder sister," she said simply and took Trisha's hand.

At that moment, the two girls' eyes met and seemed to connect deep inside. They hugged each other. One straight haired and one curly mop, but the resemblance was obvious.

And the tension in the room seemed to break everyone started talking with relief. Meera introduced Dinesh as her father, and then Eva enveloped Trisha in a hug. Everything was happening too fast, and it was more than an 11-year-old can take in.

"I'm your Mummy's friend Trisha. We studied together. Your mother wrote me a letter asking me to come to you. Do you want to hear about it?"

Trisha nodded, at a loss for words. Kong Rilang then suggested that they go for a walk while lunch was being prepared.

Both Aunty and Eva gave the lady a grateful look. It was obvious that everything was too much for Trisha and she looked overwhelmed seeing a roomful of total strangers who claimed to be her family.

So, Aunty and Uncle, along with Eva took Trisha for a walk in the Kong Rilang's back garden. The place was tranquil and there were a lot of fruit trees as well as patches of vegetables growing. It was clean and quite

neatly arranged, and above all Trisha seemed quite at home there. The surroundings seemed to calm her, and as they sat on a fallen log, Eva took her hand and began to tell her the story.

She told Trisha of how her parents, Debojit and Nisha had been her friends in Delhi, about how close they were, studying together for the exams, when suddenly Debojit had died. Eva glanced at Uncle and Aunty who gave a small nod. She didn't tell Trisha about the suicide but just said that he went to sleep and never woke up again. Eva felt that as Trisha grew older to understand, only then can she learn the truth. At present, such gruesome details are best left out as they might have a bad impact on her mind. Eva felt a strong maternal instinct towards the girl.

As she continued, Trisha listened quietly. As she heard of how Nisha gave birth to her and then left her with Mrs Lin, she asked in a small voice, "Mummy didn't love me? Is that why she left me with Mei Lin?"

Eva was at a loss for words, she didn't know how to answer that. Aunty then came and hugged Trisha, "No, darling, Mummy loved you very very much. But she didn't have a choice as your Papa had died and they were not married yet."

"Yes, sweetheart," put in Eva, her voice quivering with pain. "Mei Lin loved your mother like her own daughter and that's why she left you with her. Because she knew you would be loved and taken care of."

"And that's why before your mother died, she wrote me a letter. She made sure that I would come to you and bring you back to your Grandma and Grandpa, to your Papa's house."

"Does it mean that I would leave here now and go and live with Grandma?"

"Yes, darling. After your exams are over," replied Eva.

On hearing this, Trisha let out a whoop of joy. She jumped up, ran to Aunty and asked, "Is this true? Are you going to be my Mummy and Papa?"

Shocked at this unexpected reaction Aunty hugged her tight. Uncle too couldn't hold back his tears. "Yes, my sweetheart, we will be your Mummy and Papa. We will give you all the love in this world and never ever lose you again."

As she sat contented on the fallen log, between her grandparents, Trisha told them that ever since Mei Lin died, she felt that she was all alone in this world. Everyone who loved her had died and gone to heaven. Even though Kong Rilang and the others loved her and were very nice to her, she felt left out, a bit different from the others, she missed the love Mei Lin had for her. Mei Lin was like her own mother. So, she had prayed to God that her Mummy and Papa would come to get her. "And see, God has listened to my prayers." The innocence with which she said these words brought tears to Eva's eyes. She again marvelled at the resilience of children, their ability to simply accept things which would have been more complex in adults. Maybe when she grew up and understood things better, she would begin to question what had actually happened, she would try to find the truth, but for now she was content she had her Grandpa and Grandma with her.

They went back inside the house. As soon as they entered, Ban and Dinesh both looked up expectantly. Eva

could see the worry in their eyes, the silent questions. However, all these were swept aside as soon as they saw Trisha walking in between her grandparents, chatting animatedly with happiness radiating from all three faces. It was as if pure joy emanated from the three of them, and at that moment, all doubts Eva had if they were doing the right thing, evaporated. She was sure she had completely fulfilled the task set out for her. Her best friend's final wish that she find her daughter and take her to her grandparents. At that moment Eva felt a strange feeling, as if she could feel both Debojit and Nisha smiling and sending a thank you from beyond the grave.

EPILOGUE

It was Christmas Eve. Eva entered the living room and looked around. The huge Christmas tree looked beautiful in the corner with all the lights twinkling and lots of presents underneath. All around the room there were little touches of Christmas, all around the house in fact. The staircase was beautifully decorated with tinsel; red and green Christmas curtains, festive tablecloths and sprigs of holly in vases abounded all around the house.

The last two weeks had been a whirlwind of activity. Of course, Christmas shopping had started since the beginning of December, but Shillong in December is gripped by a festive fervour, of unending Christmas shopping. Everyone rich or poor strove to get the best outfit within their budget for the Christmas Day service. Then came the gift shopping, for friends for relatives and for the numerous secret Santa parties held across town. And there were Advent Christmas lunches or dinners, carol singing especially for the students who were leaving for Christmas in their hometowns. But it had always been a tradition to have a pre-Christmas celebration in Shillong first.

Dinesh and Meera, Uncle and Aunty along with Trisha had arrived since the 15th of December. Eva had

invited them all to spend Christmas at her place in order to give them time to get to know each other, to bond and at the same time enjoy a peaceful holiday. And what better occasion than the magical season of Christmas? Both Dinesh and Meera had been awestruck by the beauty of Shillong during Christmastime. Beginning from the first of December, it was as if all the shops and cafes had just been waiting for the day they can put up their decorations, and each shop seemed to outdo the other. There were beautifully decorated Christmas trees and Santa Clauses jostling for space in the markets, all the while with carols playing in the background. Uncle and Aunty too seemed to soak in the festive atmosphere, but Trisha seemed to be on top of the world.

In November, they had all bid a tearful goodbye to one another. Trisha had stayed for a couple of days with her grandparents in Eva's house, but she had to return to Kong Rilang's house as she was due to give her school final exams. Schools in Meghalaya held final exams in November. She was sad at the thought but soon brightened up when she was told that her grandparents would come pick her up after the exams and she would be living with them after that. And of course, the prospect of spending Christmas with Meera, Amanda and Clarissa made the wait a bit better.

After they had come to Shillong, in spite of the bitter cold, they had gone for drives to local tourists' spots, each enjoying the trip with newfound friends. They done loads of Christmas shopping, for clothes, for gifts, and of course Christmas cake, even though Eva and Ban baked scrumptious cakes at home.

Eva chuckled to herself. She remembered the previous day, as they were icing the cake, she turned around and found all four girls deep in conversation, a bowl of buttercream icing between them, and they were licking the icing with an expression of pure enjoyment.

Now with, the decorations done, the cakes ready, the presents wrapped, Eva sat back with a cup of coffee and waited for the others to come. Ban and Dinesh had taken the girls to pick up the chicken and ham for Christmas dinner the next day. The roast for Christmas Eve dinner had already been prepared and its delicious aroma permeated the house.

After dinner, they sat in the living room with the soft music of carols, telling each other stories. There were peals of laughter and smiles. The journey of these past few months had forged a deep bond between all of them. At the stroke of midnight, the whole city erupted with the ringing of church bells announcing the birth of Jesus. Ban, as the head of the family, said a word of prayer. They then had tea and cakes. And soon after, the children were eager to open their presents. As Eva watched, Ban called out names and Uncle dressed as Santa Claus gave out the presents. Eva again felt a strange sense as though Debojit and Nisha were watching over them now. She felt a sense of peace, and she felt that wherever they were in the afterlife, Debojit and Nisha were finally at peace.

Her husband came and stood beside her. No words were necessary, he understood her emotions. He put an arm around her and said softly, "And life has turned a full circle."

THE END